SUMMER IS HOME
East Texas 1950s

"The story moves so well, all the details are so right there in front of me, I can feel your version of 1950s East Texas playing before my eyes even though I've never been there in my life. All the characters are sympathetic; I loved them all, can't believe they weren't based on real people. You have quite an imagination. The dialog was spot on, I could hear it..."
Michael Davidson, publisher The Open End

"Parts I laughed. Parts I cried. The characters were so relatable. When you laugh, you feel the moment inside. And when you cry, you feel their pain. Remembrance of a time gone by. Not just a time, but a way of life."
Janice Weston Hagan, East Texan

"I appreciate your skillful style as exemplified by your characters (really strong women) and enhanced by their authentic voices along with the strong narrator dialogue you created. Overall smooth, real and tight."
Wally Aguilera, an avid reader

SUMMER IS HOME

East Texas 1950s

Mitchell Hagerstrom

Penryn Editions 2024

Summer is Home: East Texas 1950s

Copyright © 2024 by Mitchell Hagerstrom

Published by

PENRYN EDITIONS

Penryn Editions
P.O. Box 167
Queenstown, MD 21658

IBSN: 978-1-7330086-6-2

This is a work of fiction. Names, characters, places, and incidents are the product of the author's imagination or are used fictitiously, and any resemblance to actual persons, living or dead, events, or locales is entirely coincidental.

Front cover photo: Author with her father. Back cover photo: author with brother from family photo album.

AUTHOR'S NOTE

When I was living in San Francisco in 1990, I was invited one Sunday by a young workmate to ride up to Chico for a day's visit with his favorite college teacher and wife. The couple were from East Texas, from up around Marshall. They were about my age, and I found them thoroughly enchanting. During the long drive back to the city, daydreaming out the window, I began wondering what if I had spent more time with my grandparents in my mother's small East Texas hometown?

So, 1990 was the year I began working on this story, every Saturday (like a Sunday-painter). The piece enchanted me. When I visited the San Francisco main library every Sunday, there were times nothing caught my eye. What I wanted to read was the story I was writing. I continued to work fitfully on the piece for the next few decades, never losing my enthusiasm.

I have recently learned that this genre which I call fictional memoir is officially known as autofiction. Yes, the child narrator is me and the grandparents are closely modeled after my own, while the drama and events are fiction. The other characters are fictitious, and I borrowed most of their names from actual family members. The setting, the house, the small town, and the whole landscape are modeled on my remembrance of the place in the 1950s.

Taking my queue from Raymond Carver -- "A little autobiography and a lot of imagination are best", Summer is Home, offers a glimpse into what could have been.

Mitchell Anne Hagerstrom
Centreville, Maryland 2024

"We are by nature observers, and thereby learners. That is our permanent state."

– Ralph Waldo Emerson

Table of Contents

Chapter 1
Wore-out yellow hound

Thunder wakes me and I smell the coming rain. Then lightning makes the wallpaper flowers climb up and up. More thunder and more lightning. I pull the covers over my head, squeeze my eyes shut, and wrap my arms around my knees. I peek out when I hear Miss Frankie shutting the windows.

Etta? she says, you 'wake?

Yes, ma'am.

You scared?

Yes, ma'am.

Come on, then, she says, and she takes my pillow.

I trot behind her through the house, back to the room with her and Daddy Lee's bed, the small horsehair sofa, and the table for ordinary meals.

Miss Frankie goes directly to the linen press in the big closet. I wait by the foot of their bed and watch the covers rise and fall with Daddy Lee's snoring.

After Miss Frankie dresses the horsehair sofa, she pushes it across the room, smack up against their bed. She plumps my pillow and helps me over the side. After she tucks me in, she climbs over the foot of their bed and settles herself.

Then she leans down to me. Go to sleep, she whispers.

The sofa is not soft like my bed. It feels hard and itchy. For a long while I don't sleep. Thunder booms, lightning flashes in the many windows, and the rain pounds on the roof.

In the morning, I don't remember any dreams at all, and in the morning, Jewel comes calling. Although she is my auntie, I just call her Jewel. She's got on a silky kind of church dress, like the one she wore at her wedding, only this one is dark colored with little white flowers. She stands by the table and picks up the last rasher of bacon, nibbles on it.

Daddy Lee has gone off for a long visit to the bathroom. Then he will spend time in the big closet, and when he comes out his shoes will be polished and well brushed.

Jewel helps clear the table, all the while whispering to Miss Frankie who keeps lifting her shoulder, as if pushing Jewel away. Finally, she tells Jewel to hush.

In the kitchen, Miss Frankie washes the dishes. Jewel dries and puts them away. Then Miss Frankie covers the plate of leftover biscuits with the damp dish towel and sets them in the turned-off oven. Now, she says, we need to go out to the garden. She tells me to fetch a paper sack.

Yes, ma'am, I say, and I watch Jewel follow Miss Frankie out the back door.

I go to the pantry where the sun comes in a tall skinny window and puts a sparkle on the shelves of put-up peaches, tomatoes, figs, butter pickles, and jars with long fingers of pickled okra. I take a sack from the stack of them and hurry out.

In the garden the sandy dirt is rain-washed clean. I find Miss

Frankie crouched down by the tomatoes. I hand the paper sack to Jewel who tucks it under one arm, then I crouch down beside Miss Frankie, watching as she cups a tomato in her hand. When she twists it off, the plant makes a small whimpering noise, but when she turns to hand the tomato up to Jewel, I see Jewel is the one whimpering and acting as if she's cold in her silky dress.

Miss Frankie tells me to get the hoe and drag it through the corn rows. Plants can't breathe with a crust, she says. So, I get the hoe and drag it behind me through the corn rows. Then I hear Daddy Lee calling me.

I peek through the corn stalks to Miss Frankie, and she nods. I drop the hoe and run to the gate. Daddy Lee takes my hand, and we walk down to the highway, then across into town.

We stop at the barber shop where a man is laid out on one of the swivel chairs and covered up to his chin with a sheet. His face is piled with soap, making him look like one of Miss Frankie's lemon meringue pies.

The barber holds a long razor, and he slaps it across a big belt. Hey, Lee, he calls out, who's that bitty thing you got wit' you?

You 'member my grandbaby, Etta?

The barber nods. Vesta's young'un, he says, and I hear Jewel's done got herself married.

Henderson boy, Daddy Lee says in a low growly voice, and I pull on his pants leg to get us to leave. As we walk off, I tell him, I'm not a baby.

But he jiggles my hand and tells me I'll always be his sugar baby.

We walk on down to the grocery store where the floors are covered with sweet smelling sawdust, and where the butcher will give Daddy Lee leftover scraps for his hounds. While Daddy Lee talks with the butcher, I stand next to the candy counter, taking big breaths, smelling the chocolate through the wrappers. Then

I look up and inspect the bunch of bananas hanging from the ceiling. They're getting too black to eat and I think I can see a spider's hairy legs sticking out. Jewel says that bananas come from a place where spiders are as big as salad plates.

Daddy Lee takes my hand again and we go on to the drug store. There's a soda fountain, but we don't get any because Miss Frankie's fixing dinner. At the back of the store is the post office and a wall of little glass doors. Daddy Lee watches me find our box along the bottom row, then he helps me twist the numbers. The box opens and he reaches in, takes the letters, and goes back up front to buy a newspaper.

While he talks to the fella up there, I walk up and down, peeking in through the little glass doors. In the room behind are shelves of boxes wrapped in brown paper and tied around with string. There's a lady back there, sitting on a tall stool. I see a man come up behind her and yank her apron ties. She turns and swats at him. I see her surprised look as she starts to tumble off the stool, but the man reaches out and grabs her arms to save her. She falls against him, and her red-painted mouth smears itself against his collar. When she pushes him away, she's laughing.

I run to find Daddy Lee. He's out on the sidewalk and talking to some fellas sitting on the bench. I listen as they talk about dogs and lumber and the new tomato shed by the railroad tracks. Finally, Daddy Lee takes my hand, and we walk home.

While I help Miss Frankie set the table, Daddy Lee sits on the horsehair sofa, reading the newspaper. For dinner there's fried chicken, blackeye peas, cornbread, sliced tomatoes, tea for them, and sweet milk for me.

When Daddy Lee puts down his paper and comes to the table, we all set to eating and I heap my plate with peas.

Take some chicken, he says.

I tell him I only like peas, but he reaches over and gives me both the gizzard and the heart.

She won't want that, Miss Frankie says.

But I pick up the gizzard and nibble around the edges.

After a bit, Miss Frankie goes to the kitchen and comes back with a glass of buttermilk for Daddy Lee. Then she tells him Jewel might come stay a while. Just for a while, she says as she fusses with her food, not looking at him.

Time you stop babying that gal, he says, sounding put out. Time she gets used to things being different. He reaches for another piece of chicken.

I eat my peas and some cornbread.

Then Daddy Lee says, I got's to go out to Cole's. Etta, here, can come wit' me.

Miss Frankie sets down her fork. Lee, she says, should you really be taking Etta?

Eat, he says to her.

We all eat and say nothing.

When I finish my peas, I pick up the heart and bite off the bottom tip. I can see there's an empty hollow that runs right up the middle of it.

After dinner, Daddy Lee takes his afternoon nap on the long sofa in the front room, the newspaper over his head like a tent. I'm put down for a nap in my own room.

For a while I inspect the prints on the quilt, picking out the ones I like best. Then I search the wallpaper, trying to find one flower different from the others. Then I pretend to walk on the ceiling. A mud-dauber bounces against the window screen looking for a way in, and I can hear Miss Frankie in the kitchen, humming church songs to herself as she washes the dishes.

Going out to Cole's, Daddy Lee lets me ride in the bed of the pickup. Sitting back there all I can see are the tops of trees, clouds, and sky. The dead flowers that fall into the truck bed while it's parked under the mimosa fly up and blow away like butterflies.

After a long bouncing ride, the pickup skids into Cole's yard. When Daddy Lee turns off the motor, I can hear the barking and howling of his hounds. They know the sound of the pickup and are happy about getting the butcher's scraps Daddy Lee brings them.

I stand up so I can see what's going on. Cole comes from the barn and walks over. He pokes at his hat with one finger, lifting it a little, then he goes on about what last night's storm's done to his second planting. He has the squeakiest voice I ever heard on a grown man.

Never mind that, Daddy Lee says. How's that dog doing?

Cole shakes his head.

Daddy Lee hands Cole the package from the butcher, then he lifts me out of the bed and puts me up front. You wait here, he tells me, and he shuts the pickup door.

I kneel on the seat so I can watch what's going on, and I see an old, yellow-colored hound drag herself out from under the porch. She stands up on wobbly legs. Her skin hangs loose on her bones, her tail never wags, and when she tries to walk, she falls over, rolls onto her back, and shuts her eyes.

The hound pack, from the pen behind the barn, keeps on howling. I can hear the angry sound of Daddy Lee's voice but not what he's saying. Cole goes quickly into the house and comes back directly with a gun. He hands it to Daddy Lee.

Then Cole scoops up the yellow-colored hound and carries her off. Daddy Lee follows.

Cole's three boys, the littlest in nothing but a striped T-shirt, come over to the pickup. The biggest one climbs up on the running board and hangs in the window. Gimme some candy, he says, or I'll give you a sock in the head.

I scoot over behind the steering wheel, away from him. Then I hear the squeak of a screen door, and all the boys go running off. Cole's wife comes out onto the porch. She's wearing men's overalls way too big for her. Honey, she calls to me, you wanna glass a water?

I shake my head. No, ma'am, I call to her, and I look down until I hear her go back inside. Then I hear the gun go off, and the hound pack hushes dead quiet.

On the way home I sit up front with Daddy Lee. He drives so fast I feel as though we might be flying. On some bumps the pickup flies off the ground and lifts me up off the seat. It makes my stomach hurt and feel good at the same time.

When Daddy Lee parks back under the mimosa, the sun is getting low. Miss Frankie's out in the side yard watering her flowers. A piece of light has caught itself on the silver clip in her hair.

Daddy Lee goes straight into the house, throwing the screen door wide open. It shuts with a bang and then bounces again and again with smaller and smaller bangs.

I go up to Miss Frankie and tell her Daddy Lee shot that dog.

Poor thing was wore out, she says. Now, move that hose over to Lowell Thomas, will you. Come a rain, seems he wants even more water.

There weren't any funeral, I say, as I stick the hose under the rose bush with yellow flowers.

Miss Frankie shakes her head. Don't know what to do about those cannas, she says, flinging her hand up toward the chicken yard fence. Been hardly a bloom all summer. Maybe they're wore out.

Is my mama wore out? I ask.
She pulls me against her leg, cups her hand under my chin and lifts my face toward hers. Your mama's tired, she says, but she's not wore out. When she's had a good rest, your daddy's gonna come fetch you.

But I don't wanna leave, I say. Not ever.

She tells me to hush and go get washed up. She says Jewel made cobbler and I can have some if I eat my supper proper. As I walk toward the house the kitchen light comes on and there in the window is Jewel. For a tiny minute I think it's my mama.

Chapter 2
Mama's Broken Heart

Before my daddy comes for me, he gets killed in a car accident. Jewel stays with me, while Daddy Lee and Miss Frankie drive up to Iowa for the funeral. They bring my mama back. Dr. Moss comes and gives her something to make her stop crying. When they let me see her, she's sleeping.

The next day the house fills up with relatives. They come bringing covered dishes and wearing Sunday clothes. I sit and twirl on the piano stool and everyone comes over and pats my head.

Miss Frankie and a pile of lady relatives stay busy in the kitchen, fixing dinner rolls and such. My mama stays in her room, and everyone whispers that her heart is broken. I know they mean that whatever had filled up the hole in the middle has spilled out.

Through the see-through curtains on the glass doors, I see Jewel out on the brick porch. She's talking to Charlie Henderson, and she's got on one of Daddy Lee's old coats, her arms crossed to hold it closed.

As he talks, Charlie Henderson walks with his hands in his

pockets, looking down as if he's reading something written on the bricks. Jewel doesn't look at him much. After a while, he throws up his hands and walks off around the house, comes in the front door, and sits down on the long sofa between Cousin Valentine and Uncle Virgil, my very oldest uncle.

I watch for Jewel to come inside. Instead, she goes over and leans up against the butane tank. I make a final spin on the piano stool, then go off through the kitchen full of ladies, take the red car blanket off the trunk near the back door, and go out.

Behind us the Vermilion's are burning leaves and the air smells of smoke. I wrap the blanket around me like an Indian. It goes all the way to the ground and keeps my legs warm. I hear folks talking in the garden and peek through the fence slats. It's Daddy Lee and Uncle Lum. They're talking and passing a bottle back and forth, taking sips.

I head for the butane tank and when Jewel sees me, she calls, Come 'ere, you, and she lifts me up onto the tank. Then she climbs on behind me and we ride the tank like cowboys. She puts her arms around me and hugs me so tight I can feel how big her stomach is. It was Jewel who told me the reason my mama is tired but not wore out is because she lost the baby in her stomach. Now there's a baby in Jewel's stomach.

You remember your daddy? Jewel asks, her breath warming my neck.

Some, I say. I remember that sometimes his face was scratchy, and that when he laughed, I could see a gold tooth way in the back.

Your mama was just nuts about him, Jewel says. Don't think this town ever saw a girl so nuts about some fella. And him, too. He came down here a calling on some other girl, but he took one look at your mama, and that was that. It scares me just to think about it.

I never knew Jewel to be scared of anything, not thunder or lightning or mean dogs or haunts or snakes. You scared of Charlie Henderson? I ask.

That's entirely different, she says, snorting in my ear like a horse. Then she tells me that when she and my mama were little like me, their mama died, and Daddy Lee's heart was broken. But not long after, Daddy Lee and Miss Frankie got married and she made everything alright. Then she tells me she thinks my mama is planning on going back to live with my up-north grandmother. She says if I want to stay here a while longer, she will help me tell them.

Is that what you want, Etta?

I nod.

Just for a little while, we'll tell them.

Then Daddy Lee comes from the garden and hollers at us to get our behinds off that butane tank before we catch a death of cold. We scoot off the tank, and Jewel goes inside with them, but I hang back.

The grass in the side yard is brown and crunchy. Early that morning Miss Frankie had wrung three chickens, and here and there are splotches of blood from when they went dancing around without their heads. The cannas have been cut back, dug up, and put back in again. Lowell Thomas has yellow leaves, and the coral vine has been pulled off the fence.

Lifting the latch to the chicken yard gate, I go in. There are only a few chickens scratching and pecking around, and I don't see the rooster anywhere. The clothesline is empty. I walk over to the fig tree where the horny toads live. Sometimes Jewel catches one and holds it close for me to see and pet its back, then she lets it go.

Out of the corner of my eye I see the rooster hop out of the chicken house door. I see him see me, and I see the mean look in his eyes. As I run toward the gate, I hear him coming after me, his wings flapping. I yell for him to stop, and I push and push against the gate for it to open, but he keeps thumping my back and trying to get my legs. I know he is trying to kill me because Miss Frankie wrung three hens that morning and that was too many.

For a moment the rooster stops and struts away, and I call and call for someone to help me, but nobody comes. Then he sees me looking around at him and he comes flying back at me. It begins to get dark. I know that rooster would kill me if I didn't have that red blanket wrapped around me.

Finally, Daddy Lee is there, telling me to move back so he can open the gate. When I tell him I want him to kill that rooster, he says I'm a durn fool. And when he carries me inside, I'm crying. I see the lady relatives go tsk-tsk behind their teeth, and I hear them whisper I'm a poor thing who misses her daddy.

Jewel puts me in the tub to warm me up, then helps me into my flannel pajamas. Miss Frankie sets me a place at the table in the back room. When I've eaten some of this and some of that from the covered dishes, Jewel puts me to bed on a pallet in my mama's room. My own bed is needed for Cousin Valentine and her husband who drove down from Athens. There's another pallet for Jewel as her bed is needed for Uncle Lum and Aunt Bessie who drove all the way from Dallas. Uncle Virgil will sleep on the front room sofa.

My mama's room smells of floor wax and furniture polish from the good cleaning Jewel gave it. I can hear from far away the sound of folks talking. I get up and go to look at my mama. It's very dark and when I lean over, I can hear a small noise underneath her sleeping, like the sound of a tiny kitten mewing. I pick up my pillow and go down the hall to the back room where

I find Jewel and Uncle Luke alone at the table. The big dining room table must have been too full to hold them.

I want to sleep here, I say, and settle myself on the horsehair sofa.

Here? says Uncle Luke, my uncle who has only one arm. Jewel gets up and brings me a quilt. You want some more to eat? she asks.

I shake my head and settle myself.

I'd like another dinner roll, Uncle Luke says, and perhaps another piece of ham.

Jewel goes to the kitchen and comes back. She butters a roll and cuts the ham into small pieces.

Where's that husband of yours? he asks her.

He's here somewhere.

Where?

In there, she says, in the front room.

I hear you been staying here.

I'm feeling a bit delicate these days.

Guess I did hear that.

I know what folks are saying, Uncle Luke, but really, if there was a shotgun at my wedding, it was just as much on me as it was on him.

Charlie's a good boy.

Yes, I know. And young'uns need both parents.

Seems the best way.

What about Etta here, Jewell says. No parents at all. One dead and gone to heaven and the other wishing she was dead and gone to heaven.

Kinda peculiar family we got here, he says. Most ever'one's moved off and don't come back 'xcepting for funerals.

Maybe this is a good place to move away from, Jewel says.

You planning on moving off? he asks.

No, she says, I ain't planning any such thing.

I snuggle down under the quilt. I had been at Jewel's wedding, but I hadn't seen any guns there.

Whose coleslaw is this? Uncle Luke asks.

Aunt Mae's, Jewel tells him.

A mite sweet, he says, but Mae is partial to sweet.

Jewel laughs. Miss Frankie swears Aunt Mae puts a bit of sugar in everything, even her mashed potatoes.

Mae was a fine-looking woman in her day.

So, they say. Wish she would have come today.

She's rather delicate herself, Uncle Luke says. She don't like being around such sadness.

On and on they go, talking about this and that, and finally their words make no sense at all. I scrunch down into my pillow. While I sleep, Daddy Lee lifts me up and puts me on the camel. I can feel its fuzzy hair against my legs. He hands me the reins.

Chapter 3
Water Moccasin Hunt

My mama went to live with my up-north grandmother.

Jewel's baby, Jackson Parker, got born, and just as Jewel promised, she helped me to stay.

On the day for going out to open the lake house, Miss Frankie fixes pimento cheese sandwiches. I help Jewel pack diapers and things. Daddy Lee sits on the horsehair sofa jiggling Jackson Parker on his knees. Jackson Parker's head wobbles around, and Jewel keeps telling Daddy Lee to be careful. Squeaky dances around the room. She's Daddy Lee's dog, a small black one with gold-colored eyebrows and small, pointy teeth when she smiles. She lives with us and not out with Daddy Lee's hound pack at Cole's.

Going out to the lake, I ride with Daddy Lee and Squeaky in the pickup. Jewel, Miss Frankie, and Jackson Parker go ahead in the Buick. The pickup is slower than the Buick, especially with Jewel driving, and because Daddy Lee likes to play games. He turns off the motor at the top of hills and we see how far the pickup will roll before it stops.

We're heading to Daddy Lee's fishing camp. I know, from Daddy Lee telling me, how once upon a time some fellas who own the land made the lake by building a big dam and then just waited for rain and streams and springs to fill it. Between summers only Daddy Lee and Miss Frankie come out. They set trotlines for catfish or go gigging for frogs.

When we get there, a spooky gray fog is sitting on the water. Daddy Lee parks near the house, next to the Buick. He sends Squeaky to Miss Frankie and tells her to lock her inside, so she won't go running off. Then Daddy Lee and I go directly down to the lake. The water, slapping and sucking around the boathouse sounds like haunts.

Up against the front of the boathouse is a bin for growing worms. The dirt in it is soft and crumbly, full of old coffee grounds. I dig my hands in. It feels like digging into a devil's food cake, except for the tangle and wiggle of hundreds of millions of worms.

When Daddy Lee unlocks the boathouse door, I wipe my hands on my britches and follow him inside. He pulls a rope that opens the boat door and light comes in, showing it is only a place that smells of fish and lakeweed, and there are no haunts at all.

Daddy Lee's boat floats on the water. On the walls are oars and fishing poles, and a canoe is hanging way up high up. From off the wall Daddy Lee lifts an old broom handle. Stuck in one end are two nails, sharpened into points. Come on, he says, and I follow him outside.

Jewel is sitting in a sling chair between the house and the road. She has a diaper draped over one shoulder and down her front, underneath she's feeding Jackson Parker. Miss Frankie is standing on the front steps of the house and reaching across with a broom, dusting the window screens, and knocking down cobwebs from under the eaves. She stops when she sees us and calls out:

You leave Etta here!

You let that dog out, Daddy Lee calls back, and Squeaky begins to bark.

I see Miss Frankie making her mouth all tight, but after a minute she reaches behind her and opens the house door.

Squeaky comes flying out and runs to us.

The three of us walk off along the mud bank. Squeaky's in front, running, stopping, sniffing, and growling. And Daddy Lee keeps saying over and over in a low, growly voice: That's it, Squeaky, get that varmint.

The hairs on Squeaky's back are standing straight up, and my own hair begins to tingle at the back of my neck.
Squeaky's so little, I say. How come we don't use one of your hound dogs?

Daddy Lee tells me hounds are for real hunting and don't know a thing about snakes except to stay outta their way. Squeaky'll do just fine, he says.

Up over the other side of the lake the sun begins to bust through the fog. All the trees have tiny green leaves, except for the dead ones sticking out of the water. From across the lake comes the sound of ducks quacking and frogs croaking.

Back! Daddy Lee shouts, and I stumble backward, away from the water moccasin he flipped from the water's edge with the pointy broom handle.

The snake begins to squirm, but then Squeaky grabs it. She shakes it, her whole body shakes it, and then she flings it away from the lake up toward the dirt road. And before it can sneak off, she has it again, shaking and flinging it over and over, and all the while Daddy Lee keeps saying in that low, growly voice, get it, Squeaky, get that varmint. If it's flung near him he kicks at it or pokes at it until Squeaky has it again.

Finally, the snake no longer moves. Squeaky sits back, pant-

17

ing like summer, and Daddy Lee stabs the snake over and over with the pointy broom handle. You take this one, he says to me, and go on back.

I look down at the snake.

Go on, he says, take it by the tail.

I reach down and take hold of the tail. It feels alive and all the way back to the house I walk sideways so I can keep an eye on it. Well, Miss-Missy, Miss Frankie says, her hands on her hips.

Squeaky did it, I say. All by herself.

Jewel comes over. She hands Jackson Parker to Miss Frankie. Sure is a big 'un, she says, taking the tail from me.

I follow her over to the sweetgum, where she flings it over the lowest branch. Then she takes my hand, and we walk a ways off, turn and look back. Jewel explains that if you take the first one of the season and hang it where all the others can see it, they'll keep clear of our place.

For lunch there's a big jar of sweet tea, canned potato sticks, and pimento cheese sandwiches. Then Miss Frankie tells Jewel to be sure and put me down for a nap, and she and Daddy Lee go off in the boat.

Jewel puts Jackson Parker down for a nap, but not me. She tells me we'll make a stroller for him and when he wakes up from his nap, we'll take a walk.

She takes a wooden wheelbarrow from beside the house and dusts it off. The wheel makes a loud noise.

He won't like that, I say.

We walk down to the boathouse to look for an oil can, but Jewel can't find one. I follow her back to the house where she puts some shortening to melt in a skillet.

We could just carry him, I say.

Yes, she says, but it's more fun making something. And she shows me how once the house had been smaller, and she shows me where Daddy Lee made the roof wider and pushed the walls out. She shows me the old wall's shingles beside the bunk bed.

When we go back outside Squeaky comes with us. She thinks there's something in that skillet for her. Jewel pours the shortening on the wheel, and it stops making any noise. Then she cuts some long whips from a beautyberry bush and fixes them across the top. She ties one of Jackson Parker's baby blankets over them and puts two pillows inside. She tells me when Jackson Parker wakes up, we'll put him in what we built and go for a walk. Squeaky will come with us.

And that's what we do. We walk all the way to the far end before the road turns back toward the big dam. Jewel says we'll come back in the summer to see this end of the lake. She says it gets full of big lily pads with beautiful flowers on long skinny necks.

When Miss Frankie and Daddy Lee get back, they have a string of perch. Miss Frankie goes up to the house to start the cornbread and Jewel goes up to feed Jackson Parker. Daddy Lee sets about cleaning the fish.

I didn't take any nap, I tell him.

He nods but doesn't say anything.

I helped Jewel fix the wheelbarrow for Jackson Parker to ride in and then we went for a walk. Squeaky watched for snakes. We saw some duck eggs in the tall grass, but we didn't take any.

He keeps cleaning the fish, scraping the scales off with his knife, flipping the guts into the bucket, but I'm sure he is listening.

We looked in the window of that house up the road. There were boxes of saltines and little cans of Vienna sausage on the shelf by the stove. Jewel and Jackson Parker are gonna stay out here all summer, and I want to, too.

Daddy Lee stops messing with the perch and shakes the knife at me. Jewel is not staying out here, he says. She's going back and live with her husband and stop this nonsense.

Charlie Henderson is nonsense, I say. Me and Jewel and Jackson Parker are gonna live out here and make things, like how you pushed the walls out and made the house bigger. And we're gonna visit Mother Nature and Jewel's gonna show me the best way to put worms on a fishhook, but we'll fish from the pier and not out in the boat 'cause me and Jackson Parker don't know how to swim, and if the boat turns over Jewel can't save us both.

Daddy Lee says nothing, but I can tell he doesn't mean no. He hands me the fish he cleaned and tells me to take them up to the cornbread maker. I think it is a fine joke, him calling Miss Frankie that.

Me and Jewel and Jackson Parker and Squeaky get to stay at the house that night. I help Miss Frankie put sheets on the big bed where Jewel and Jackson Parker will sleep. Then we put sheets on the bottom bunk. I can't sleep on the top one because I might roll off.
After Daddy Lee and Miss Frankie leave, Jewel fixes us a supper of canned tomato soup and some potato sticks. The house has only a cold-water shower. Jewel turns it on, and we stick our feet in, then we wash our hands and faces. In the summer, Jewel tells me, we'll take our baths in the lake.

Squeaky settles herself on my feet to keep them warm. It seems darker than I ever remember. I hear frogs croaking, whip-poor-wills calling each other, and all kinds of varmints rustling in the bushes.

I reach out and touch the shingles of the old wall. You awake? I call in a loud whisper.

Uh huh, Jewel answers.

What else can we make?

What's it you want?

Can we make a bicycle?

Probably not, she says. Anyway, you're too little for a bicycle. But tomorrow we can go fishing. I'll teach you a fancy way of putting worms on the hook.

From the pier, I remind her, not from the boat.

Jackson Parker makes a noise. What's that? Jewel says to him, you hungry again already?

Squeaky wiggles herself up closer to me. Fish for the cornbread maker, I whisper to her. She yawns right in my face, and I can still smell that old snake on her breath.

Chapter 4
Wash Day, At Uncle Luke's

Monday is wash day. For the white things, the water is boiling hot, and Miss Frankie uses a big wooden stick to stir the sheets and pillow slips, then the towels, wash rags and dish rags. Later Miss Frankie will put Jackson Parker's diapers in that same hot water. The paddle in the machine swishes back and forth, and the whole thing shakes and jiggles. Like a coochie-coochie dancer, Jewel says, wiggling her behind.

Using the big wooden stick, Miss Frankie stirs the hot laundry and then lifts it, piece by piece, into the wringer. Jewel turns the handle, and the clean things drop into the rinse tub, where Jewel pushes it down. She stirs it around with the big stick, then pokes it into the wringer, making it fall into the bluing tub. I help by putting my hands into the cool, sky-blue water, floating my hands around like birds playing in the clouds.

Jewel swivels the wringer around and Miss Frankie pokes the laundry through again and it falls into a big basket. When they carry the basket out to the clothesline in the chicken yard, I follow them. The rooster keeps away when grown-ups are around. I watch them hang the sheets, then Miss Frankie goes back to tend to the diapers, and I hand the pillow slips and such to Jewel and she pins them.

Then we go back to the washroom to put the diapers through the wringer and into the rinse, then into the bluing tub, and then into the basket. After that Miss Frankie puts our everyday clothes into the tub while Jewel and I go out to hang up the diapers. A regular assembly line, Jewels says. Like working in a factory. I'm not sure what an assembly line or a factory is.

When everything is clean and hanging on the lines, the tubs get emptied onto the floor where the drain takes it out through the lean-to where potatoes and such are stored in bins of sand. Then, like a small creek, the water goes under the clotheslines and across to the fig tree, then under the fence into the Vermillion's back yard where it waters their pear and pecan trees.

From a long way off we hear Jackson Parker crying. Jewel says she knows he can't be hungry. She nudges me to go see what's going on. I find Jackson Parker standing against the side of the horsehair sofa, not knowing how to get down. Daddy Lee was supposed to be watching him, but he's sitting at his big desk in the hallway and doing his numbers. He is working so hard he doesn't hear Jackson Parker crying.

I crouch down and then stand, crouch and stand, showing Jackson Parker how. Finally, he lets go and gets down just fine. I give him a toy truck and then I go to watch Daddy Lee. I stand by his chair. He tells me he is counting the numbers of what is for store-bought groceries, what's for butane, for chicken feed, and for gasoline for the Buick and the pickup.

How is it, Daddy Lee? I ask.

He lifts me up onto his lap and shows me the numbers, which are for paying taxes, which money comes from Cole and others who farm Daddy Lee's land, and which is from his own work.

I know that Daddy Lee gets paid for traipsing through the piney woods and counting trees, then telling folks how many sawed boards those trees will make. Daddy Lee has a special talent. I hope that when Jackson Parker and I get bigger we will find out what our talents are. Miss Frankie's talent is for making things alright, and Jewel hopes her own talent is for making ladies' hair curly.

On wash days we have leftovers from Sunday dinner. Today, there's slices of roast chicken, soft rolls, English peas, tomatoes, and pickled okra. When we finish, we set out to Uncle Luke's who has been feeling poorly. We all ride in the Buick, but Squeaky stays home.

I wear the beautiful brown coat with a big velvet collar my mama sent me, even though it is not a very cold day. Miss Frankie says the coat is much too grand for anything but special occasions. To me, going to visit Uncle Luke is a special occasion.

Uncle Luke never had a wife or any children, and his house has only two rooms. One for sleeping and the other has kitchen stuff on one side with a small table with two chairs. On the other side are another two chairs with cushions near the heating stove and the radio. In the other room is a bed, a dresser, and a mirror on the wall. There's a tiny door to a tiny closet, and another tiny door to a toilet. All the walls of the house are plain wood without any wallpaper, but there are flowers on the linoleum.

One of Uncle Luke's arms was cut off in a sawmill accident a long, long time ago, but he is famous for the large yellow clingfree peaches in his orchard, and he grows winter greens. The very back of his yard is filled with blackberry bushes. His chickens are banties because Uncle Luke says he could never eat a whole regular chicken. Instead of a chicken yard, he keeps them in a small shed with one side covered in wire fence. There is also a door for the egg gatherer to get in and out and for sweeping up the chicken-poo.

When we get there, Aunt Mae is sitting by Uncle Luke's bed and working on her tatting. Aunt Mae is the sister of my real grandma and not at all related to Uncle Luke who is Miss Frankie's older brother. We have a great many relatives, and I am still figuring out who belongs to Daddy Lee, who to Miss Frankie, and who to my real grandma who died and went to heaven.

Jewel finds a plucked banty in the sink and sets to making it into soup. Daddy Lee and Miss Frankie take the two straight chairs into the bedroom. I'm told to keep Jackson Parker out of trouble. When he gets loud, Miss Frankie gets up and closes the bedroom door.

How come Aunt Mae is here? I ask Jewel. She's not related to Uncle Luke.

Jewel tells me Aunt Mae and Uncle Luke are special friends. He grows the peaches, and she puts them up.

And the blackberries?

Yes, and the blackberries.

But she's not staying over, is she? There's only one bed and it's too small.

You are too nosy, Etta, Jewel says. Now keep Jackson Parker away so I can finish this soup.

I find a chewed-up dog ball and wonder who could have left it here. Then I get Jackson Parker to sit for a bit while I roll it to him and show him how to push it back to me. When Jewel tells me to go get her a pinch off a certain plant around the back of the house, I put on my beautiful coat, and hurry out.

The plant is just where Jewel says it is and I take a pinch. When I walk past the bedroom window I peek inside. They are all just sitting there. But when I get back inside, I see the bedroom door is open and Aunt Mae has come out and is drawing a big basin of water from the kitchen sink. She then puts it on the stove. I give the pinch of leaves to Jewel who puts them in the cooking pot. Jackson Parker is riding her hip.

He won't be quiet, Jewel says, not even when Aunt Mae tickles his neck.

Jewel goes to tell Daddy Lee to take them home. While they are gone, Aunt Mae takes the big basin of water into the bedroom. She doesn't shut the door, and I can peek around the corner and watch as they take off Uncle Luke's pajama top. I can see where his arm ends, the skin tucked up and wrapped in on itself.

When Miss Frankie wipes his chest with the water, he opens his eyes a bit, then shuts them tight. All the while, I hear Miss Frankie humming church songs, so softly I almost can't hear. Then Aunt Mae spies me out of the corner of her eye and tells me to go outside and play.

So, I put my coat on and go out and around the back. First, I look at the banties. I poke a stick through the wire fence, and they try to eat it. Then I go all the way back to the blackberry bushes. There aren't any berries, but underneath I find a bunch of grass that looks like a nest, and in it is an egg. Not a banty egg but a big one.

I put the egg in my coat pocket with my hand wrapped around it. Then I run to see if it's alright to go inside to show them. Just as I make the turn around the corner of the house, I slip and fall flat out. The egg breaks and there is the most awful smell. I pull my hand from my pocket and wipe it on the grass. I try to pull out as much of the goo as I can and keep wiping my hand on the grass. Someone, but I'm not sure who, is going to be fierce because I wrecked my beautiful coat.

Through the bedroom window I can see Miss Frankie carrying the basin back to the kitchen. Aunt Mae is still sitting on her chair, but her hands are quiet, not doing her tatting. Uncle Luke is wearing a different pajama top.

When Miss Frankie comes back, she sits down on the side of the bed. With her eyes closed, she puts her hands on Uncle Luke's head, then moves them to cover his ears, then around his neck, then onto his chest. From the way she is holding her mouth I know she is humming church songs.

When I hear the Buick coming back from taking Jewel and Jackson Parker home, I hurry to meet Daddy Lee and ask him to please take me home.

Come on, he says, and I run to the other side of the Buick and climb in.

I roll the coat into a ball and when Daddy Lee asks ain't I cold, I tell him I ain't. I tell him I've been running, and I feel hot. When he lets me off at the house, I go directly in and hide the coat in the bottom of a closet. Then I double, double wash my hands with soap and hot, hot water. But that rotten egg stink is still stuck in my nose.

I go looking for Jewel and find her changing Jackson Parker on the big bed in the back room. I climb up and sit next to him. I tell Jewel what I saw and ask her what Miss Frankie was doing. Jewel stops and takes the diaper pins from her mouth. She tells me Miss Frankie was taking away Uncle Luke's sickness.

How?

Jewel lifts her shoulders. Nobody knows how. She just does it. Of course, it doesn't always work. Miss Frankie's not Jesus Christ, you know.

Up in my nose I can still smell that awful rotten egg even though I washed and washed. I stick my hands under me. Where does it go? I ask Jewel.

Where does what go?

The sickness.

I don't know, Jewel says, maybe Miss Frankie takes it up into herself? Only it never makes her sick.

I almost tell Jewel about my coat when Jackson Parker pees right up into his own face. Jewel squeals, Jackson Parker yelps, and I laugh. Jewel wipes his face and finishes changing him. Boys are like that, she xplains. They just can't help themselves.

Chapter 5
Library Visit, Reading

The day Jewel takes the Buick, and we go to Tyler, JP rides on a pillow on my lap. I can't see, but I know outside are just trees and more trees. When we arrive, I scooch JP and the pillow off me toward Jewel, so I can peek out the window. Tyler has beautiful streets made of bricks, same as Miss Frankie's Methodist Church, and when I say this, Jewel explains that East Texas red dirt makes good bricks, it being full of iron and clay. She says a relative of Daddy Lee's grandfather had a Tyler brick factory once upon a time and that all these bricks probably came from there.

Then Jewel ticks off on her fingers what all we have to do in Tyler.

First, we go to a place that will clean my beautiful coat that's riding on the back seat in a brown paper sack. It no longer stinks, but the pocket is still full of smashed duck egg. Jewel explains that a drycleaner uses chemicals instead of water to clean things and something like that broken egg in the pocket needs those chemicals. I don't understand but I don't say anything. After

Jewel leaves the coat there, we drive to the library and Jewel explains it's a place where books live and the folks there will let us borrow some if we promise to bring them back.

Jewel carries JP on her hip. The building is made of bricks just like the streets, but the steps are made of stone. I see a dip in the middle. Jewel says the dip comes from so many people walking up them year after year.

Jewel shows me where the picture books are, then she scurries off to find a place to change JP. She tells me to pick out any I would like to take home. When she comes back, she puts JP in my lap and goes off to look for a book that tells her where to find the Tyler beauty school.

Jewel has decided that soon, when JP doesn't need to get milk from her bosom, she's going to go to beauty school so she will have a way of making a living. I know from hearing Miss Frankie and Daddy Lee talking that Charlie Henderson sends money to buy what JP needs. But Jewel still wants to go to beauty school. Then Miss Frankie can give JP cow's milk and mashed up food just like we eat. But first, Jewel has to get some papers and information from the school.

I sit on the floor and take books from the shelf, open them, and show them to JP who is not interested. A lady comes up and asks if she can help me. I tell her I like stories and my auntie and my granma will read them to me if I can take them home.
And is this your little brother? The lady asks.

I tell her JP is my cousin and his real name is Jackson Parker, but anymore we just call him JP. We are waiting for his mama, my auntie.

I am pleased JP is acting proper, just looking around and admiring everything. Seems he likes new places.
The lady hands me a book about a girl named Madeline who lives in Paris. She tells me Paris is a big city in France, which is another

country far away. Then she gives me a book by a doctor which she says is silly and will make me laugh.

When Jewel comes, I show her the books the lady helped me find. Jewel puts JP on her hip, and we go looking for something for Miss Frankie. Jewel tells me Miss Frankie used to be a schoolteacher, and when Jewel goes to beauty school and has to go up to Tyler, she will bring back books for both me and Miss Frankie every week.

JP is getting fussy. When we leave Tyler, Jewel finds a place to park the Buick off the road. It's in the trees where no one can see us. Then she feeds JP from her bosom while I look at the pictures in the books. There are words at the bottom of the pages, but I don't know what they say.

Then we eat the baloney sandwiches Miss Frankie fixed for us and take sips from a jar of sweet tea.

When we get home, Jewel parks the Buick under the carport. Miss Frankie comes from the garden. I show her all the books. She seems mighty pleased. I mean, she smiles real big and gives me a hug.

She tells me to put them inside on the trunk and to come help her in the garden. I leave the books and go back with her to the garden. She has been digging up the first crop of potatoes.

She tells me these potatoes are for now, for this spring and the summer, and that the second planting of regular potatoes will be for the winter and for as long as they last.

Ain't you gonna put them up in jars for the pantry? I ask.

They's too big for jars, she says, and tells me when she flicks them up, I'm supposed to make sure they get on the gunny sack, then she'll drag them to the shed.

So, Miss Frankie forks and I grab. Soon there's a big pile on the gunny sack.

The potatoes are red ones and remind me of the pretty red brick roads in Tyler, but I don't say anything about that. Ain't we gonna wash 'em off? I ask.

No, Missy, Miss Frankie says, leave the dirt on. We'll wash 'em just 'fore we cook and eat 'em. She pulls the gunny sack out the garden gate and up to the chicken yard. She opens the gate, looks around and tells me the rooster is hiding out.

I follow her into the shed next to the laundry room. Inside the lean-to are bins of sand. Miss Frankie shows me how to push the sand to one side and lay a row of potatoes, and push sand back over them, then more rows of potatoes and more sand. When we have buried all the potatoes from the gunny sack, Miss Frankie says we gotta go back for more.

We go back to the garden two more times. Then she hands me the pitch fork and tells me to prop it against the fence. She grabs hold of the last gunny sack and drags it toward the garden gate, then out and up to the chicken yard gate.

I hold the gate open, and she drags the gunny sack around, past the fig tree and into the lean-to shed.

It has been a fearsome amount of work, and I can see Miss Frankie is all sweaty, but we are both smiling. Plenty to last us all summer, she says. Now, let's go get washed up for supper.

Neither one of us took a nap today.

After Miss Frankie has her bath, I use her leftover bathwater, with a bit more hot water added. Then we take ourselves to the table, Miss Frankie in her nightgown and robe and me in pajamas. Daddy Lee says he guesses the potatoes been dug.

With Miss Missy's help, Miss Frankie says.

Daddy Lee nods and I feel well praised.

Jewel brings the supper in: breakfast biscuits smothered in a goopy sauce. But I eat my fill. It ain't that bad.

Then it's teeth brushing and to bed. Miss Frankie comes with me and brings the books the library lady picked out for me.
We prop ourselves on my bed and open the first one. Before Miss Frankie starts to read I have so many questions. Where do all these little girls come from? There ain't that many little girls around here, I say.

If you was to go to school here, she tells me, you would meet other little girls. She says there were almost that many girls in her class when she first started school, and she tells me she sees many of them at church ever' Sunday.

Then Miss Frankie points at the first word and tells me what it is. Then she points to the second word and on and on. But only the first two pages, over and over, until I am reading just like I always knew how.

When Miss Frankie leaves to go back to her bed, I feel so happy knowing I know how to read, but then I remember Jewel has told me my mama says I have to go to school up north. Still, I am happy because I know how to read.

Chapter 6
Up-north Grandmother

Miss Frankie has pinned a note on the wide velvet collar ofmy brown coat that Jewel has made sure is no longer full of rotten egg stink. The note says where I am going and who will meet me at the train station. Daddy Lee is driving the Buick and Miss Frankie is riding up front. I am alone in the back with a suitcase on the seat beside me.

From the backseat windows, I can see nothing but trees. The pines are green, but the others are turning colors. Miss Frankie has explained to me that it is what certain trees do. The leaves turn colors and then brown and they all fall off. In spring they come back again, all green. I have seen that with the trees at the lake.

When we get to the train station, Daddy Lee parks the Buick and carries my suitcase up to where the train will be coming. Miss Frankie holds my hand tight and tells me over and over that everything will be alright.

When the train comes, Miss Frankie helps me up the steps and onto the train. I follow her to a little room with a sofa on each side. Daddy Lee comes and lifts my suitcase way up on a high shelf. There are windows where I can look out. Miss Frankie gives me a paper sack with things to eat and a jar of sweet tea. Both Daddy Lee and Miss Frankie sit across from me and tell me how much they love me. Daddy Lee looks so sorrowful.

Miss Frankie tells me again that I am to wait on the train until my mama comes to fetch me and that I am not to go with anyone else.

Yes, ma'am.

You understand? You stay right here until your mama fetches you?

Yes. ma'am.

My beautiful brown coat is hot, but I am too scared to take it off. I undo the buttons and open it for air. The note Miss Frankie pinned to the collar is still there. I sit and watch out the window as the whole country goes by. No one else comes to sit on the other sofa. After a while I get hungry. I eat the egg salad sandwiches Miss Frankie packed for me, and I drink the sweet tea from the jar. On and on the train goes.

After a while I lie down on the sofa and fall asleep, and when I wake it is dark. The train is no longer moving. I can hardly see anything out the windows. I sit and wait and wait. Nobody comes. I need to pee so bad that I pee into the jar where the sweet tea was.

I sleep some more and when morning comes, my mama is there. She's wearing pearls, the pearls she once told me my daddy gave her when they got married. She's crying and hugging me tight. I go with her. She brings my suitcase from off the tall shelf and the paper sack with my pee in a jar.

We leave the train, and she puts me in an automobile, much

like the Buick but only bigger and black.

I ask whose it is.

She tells me it belongs to my up-north grandmother who I don't remember, because I was just a tiny baby when I left Iowa. And that is where we are going. To her house.

Soon we are there. I have never seen such a grand house. It has a carport like at Daddy Lee's, but the house is tall. The Henderson's across the street had both a bottom and a top and stairs, but it is not grand like this. Inside the walls of the house are dark wood below and papered above with flowers. I follow her up a staircase where there are more rooms. She crosses her lips with a finger to warn me to be quiet and whispers that Grandmother Lewis is sleeping. She points to a door we pass.

Tonight, she whispers, you will sleep with me, and she takes me down the hall to a big room with a big bed and windows on the far side. She sets my suitcase on the bed, opens it, and begins taking things out.

Goodness, she says, we need to go shopping for you, need to get you some warm things. It gets cold up here.

I'm sitting on a small chair, watching, but I say nothing.

She takes my coat with the beautiful collar and hangs it in the closet. Come, she says. And I follow her farther down the hall. She shows me the bathroom. The bathtub is a big one and stands up on feet that look like the claws of a big bird, a hawk, or an eagle. She waits while I pee. Then I follow her down some other stairs, skinny ones, that lead to a kitchen.

She opens a can of chicken noodle soup, heats it on the stove, then puts it in a bowl on top of a plate and puts some saltines around it. Then she gives me a big glass of sweet milk. I watch as she fixes a tray to take up to Grandmother Lewis. The same soup and crackers but with a cup of hot tea. This is Iowa, my mama says. Folks up here don't drink sweet tea.

She waits while I finish my soup and crackers, then I follow her up the back stairs and down the hall to the room she pointed to before. My mama opens the door to the room and there is an old woman in a big bed. Many white pillows are piled behind her. She smiles sweetly at me.

Mama pulls a pillow down and sets the tray on it, then she leads me to the other side of the bed. This is your grandmother, she tells me. The old woman continues to smile sweetly.

We sit while Grandmother Lewis slurps her soup, munches her crackers, and drinks her tea. My mama talks to her, tells her about picking me up from the train and such.

When my new grandmother has finished the soup and tea, my mama takes the tray. I give a curtsy, like I'd seen in a movie Jewel took me to once, and my new grandmother waves to me like she is a queen.

As we walk down the hall back toward the kitchen stairs, my mama says I am to choose a room for my own. Holding the tray under one arm, she opens all the doors as we walk along. I peek into each one. Then I choose the smallest one, far down the hallway, across from the stairs leading down to the kitchen. Out one window of that room, I can see the roof over the kitchen porch.

My mama puts me in a school where the teachers wear long black robes, and they cover their heads with black scarfs. I understand it is the school Grandmother Lewis wants me to go to. It is not in the neighborhood, so my mama drives me every day. Both my mama and Grandmother Lewis are surprised I can read, or at least read some. I ask my mama if she can take me to a library like Jewel does. Instead, my mama goes by herself, leaving me with the housekeeper, and brings me back books. I read them to Grandmother Lewis every day after school. Being with Grandmother Lewis and reading books from the library is better than being at school.

My mama has told me that Grandmother Lewis took to her bed when my daddy died. I understand her heart was broken, and this is why my mama cannot leave her and go home.

One day in the kitchen, my mama fixes a salad, not like any salad Miss Frankie ever made, or even Jewel. I will be glad when I have learned enough in school so I can write letters and tell them all about this place.

I watch as mama tears up big lettuce leaves, such as I've never seen before, then she adds sliced olives, black ones and green ones with pimento, some chopped tomatoes, then a can of tuna. She dresses the whole thing with what she makes herself with mustard, lemon juice, and oil, scrambled fast together. She sprinkles it all with salt and pepper. Your daddy taught me this, she says.

I think it is strange, but I like it.

Then, for Christmas, my mama gives me roller skates. They latch on to my regular shoes and with a twist of a key they hold tight. She tells me to take them to the basement where the floor is smooth, all concrete, and at first to use just one skate so I get used to it. Round and round, and then with both skates. I feel I am flying.

Chapter 7
Cynthia Parker's Corn Crib

In the summer, I am allowed to come home. My mama pins a note to my red sweater, and I ride the train through fields where corn is not so high, and the closer to home we get, the taller it is. The train wanders around hills and through the piney woods. At the train depot in Tyler, Daddy Lee and Squeaky are there to collect me. We are all wearing big smiles and we share hugs all around.

At home JP doesn't seem to remember me at all. Miss Frankie puts him in a new little red wagon, and I pull him into the garden while Miss Frankie finishes her chores there. Then I pull him back to the house, and Miss Frankie carries him up the steps. JP no longer wears diapers, and he walks pretty good.

Daddy Lee and Squeaky take a walk into town to get the mail while I play with JP and Miss Frankie fixes dinner. Then Jewel comes home from her beauty shop, and it feels as if I have never been gone.

At dinner Daddy Lee talks about the roof of the shack of the fella who tends his corn and pea crops. That it has holes in it. He's the fella who keeps the mule named John Henry and who farms some of Daddy Lee's land. John Henry plows the fields and pulls the wagon to town so that the fella can get commodities and sell off what's left from the fields that Daddy Lee doesn't take.

After dinner and our naps, Jewel goes back to her shop. Miss Frankie takes out her quilt pieces and sets to work on the table while JP plays with his toys on the floor. Daddy Lee and Squeaky and I ride out to the fella's place.

I stay in the pickup while Daddy Lee talks to the fella and points to the roof. The fella nods. His place is mean looking. There's no paint on the shack and it doesn't have any windows. Then Daddy Lee and Squeaky walk off to inspect the corn crop. The old fella comes up and tips his hat to me. You's Miss Rosetta, he says. I knew yer grandma.

I look up at him and nod.

Mighty fine lady, he says, yer grandma.

About then, Daddy Lee comes back from walking the corn rows and he's more angry than I've ever seen him. He's waving a couple of corn ears and yelling that they are all trash. I can see where he's pulled down the shucks and there's puffy purplish stuff where it ought to be pretty yellow corn teeth.

Driving home Daddy Lee tells me it weren't that fella's fault. That it was just was bad weather that brung on that fungus.

The next day I ride out with Daddy Lee to see some other fellas who can fix that roof. Where we're going is up the Athens road, and the fellas who are gonna fix the roof are brothers named Joe and Jo. Miss Frankie already told me they are married to two sisters, and they all live in the same house. One Joe is Joseph, and the other Jo is Josiah. They're both Baptist preachers, but Daddy Lee says they don't have a calling right now, so they have time to fix that roof. He says he don't have a problem with them being Baptist as they are good carpenters.

Daddy Lee turns the pickup across the highway and drives uphill. He stops at the top, beside a house. I tell Daddy Lee I need to pee, and he says something to the fellas, and one of them points to around the back of the house.

Daddy Lee tells me they ain't got indoor plumbing and there's an outhouse around back. I go off thataway and find it. It's like the one at Daddy Lee's lake house, only spooky.

The door opens with a loud creak and there are spider webs everywhere. If I didn't have to pee so bad, I would surely run away. But I leave the door open, go in, turn around, drop my shorts, then my panties, and skooch up so my behind is over the hole. The whole time I'm peeing I am scared something's gonna reach up and grab me. There's a Sears catalog on the shelf beside me and I tear off a page, then ruffle it to make it softer before I wipe myself.

While I was busy, Daddy Lee walked way out back with those fellas. So, I traipse through the tall grass, heading for the back fence where Daddy Lee is standing with those fellas. All of them are looking out over the fence to where the land falls away. I hurry. I want to know what they're looking at back there.

Daddy Lee sees me coming, and when I get there, he sweeps me off my feet, lifts me high so I can look over the fence.

What is it? I ask. All I see is an old corn crib with most all the whitewash worn off. It's empty. No corn at all.

Daddy Lee tells me JP's great, great aunt Parker used to get locked in there.

The fellas, Joe and Jo, nod their heads. Yessir, she sure was. How come, I ask?

One of the fellas says it was to keep her from running away. Then he goes on and on about how when she was a little girl, not a lot older than me, the Indians kidnapped her and took her off to Comanche land and kept her there for years and years until the Texas Rangers found her. They brung her and her babe back here to her sister's farm, right over yonder. But all she wanted to do was go back and live with the Indians. So, her sister had to lock her in the crib to keep her.

Something didn't sound right to me. Why? I ask.

So she wouldn't run back and live with the Indians, says that one fella. Indians are heathens, he adds.

But I wonder why she wanted to go back to the Indians.

Going home, I ask Daddy Lee what was the name of JP's great-great-aunt.

Cynthia Ann Parker, he says.

Did you know her?

Did not, he says, only knew about her. I don't remember any Indians around here. I do remember cowboys.

I wait and say nothing, knowing he's gonna tell me more.

When I was about your age, he says, there used to be cattle drives right through town.

You saw them?

I saw them. Cattle being driven up north to the stockyards in Fort Worth, then shipped on by train to markets back east. The line of cows, with cowboys whipping them on, seemed to go on for miles and miles and my mama complained about the dust they kicked up. It was something awful.

Supper that night is my favorite, Raisin Bran and cinnamon toast, extra milk if we want, but no extra sugar on the cereal as the toast is sprinkled with brown sugar. Miss Frankie tells me to slow down, says I'll get a bellyache from eating so fast, and that young ladies don't gobble their food. Since I am not a young lady I don't care, but I pretend to listen.

All I'm wanting is to get Jewel to tell us what she knows about JP's great-great-aunt, Cynthia Ann Parker.

Turns out it's a long bedtime story, with JP getting put down in my bed and Jewel squeezing up next to us. And the big surprise is JP's great-great-aunt is the mother of a great Indian chief named Quanah Parker.

Chapter 8
Summer is Home

We make camp for the night on a ridge, using our saddles as pillows and spreading the saddle blankets to sleep on. Then we build a fire.

Open that can of beans, I say to Matt.

Matt is JP's cowboy name, and the ridge is really the crook of the chinaberry tree where Daddy Lee nailed some boards to make a flat floor. Me and Matt have a herd of cattle to get to Fort Worth and all around us are rustlers and hostile Indians.
I set about making a pot of coffee and tell Matt to go check on our horses.

JP looks down. They're okay, he says. Some sticks are nailed to the trunk for a ladder, but JP is only four and it isn't easy for him to climb up and down.

So, we eat our beans, drink the coffee, and go to sleep. When we wake up, we find the whole herd is gone. I am sure it was rustlers.

We still got our horses, Matt says.

At the bottom of the tree are Matt's palomino, a yellow

broomstick, and my silvery-brown stallion with a lock of mop-mane. We decide to break camp and head out.

Looks like they crossed the badlands, I say, pointing across the street to Hazelton's side yard, a patch of nothing but weeds and sticker-burrs.

JP looks down at his bare feet. No, he says.

We have to, Matt. We have to find that herd.

So, we start out across the Hazleton's side yard, using our horses as poles to lean on. Every step we have to stop and pull sticker-burrs from the bottom of our feet. Halfway across JP starts bawling, and by the time I reach the safety of the other side, he's hollering for Miss Frankie.

After JP gets rescued, we decide to forget about finding our cattle. I figure the rustlers had too good a head start, anyway.

Let's be Indians, JP says.

We change the names of our horses and ourselves and set about being Indians. When Miss Frankie calls us to come eat, we have almost finished gathering the fixings for Indian stew: chinaberries, torn up leaves, little black balls from the four o'clocks, and some of Daddy Lee's hot peppers stolen from the garden. But we decide to go inside for a regular dinner.

Jewel is already there. She closes her beauty shop to come home for dinner. She says she is rarely too busy. There's hardly enough ladies left in this town to keep me open, she says.

Daddy Lee is back from his walk to the post office, and there is a letter from my mama. I'm not too interested. Up north there is only that big old empty house, Grandmother Lewis who is too sick to leave her room, and Father McLaughlin who comes every Sunday to dinner. Since I live up there and only come home for summers, I know that nothing much changes up north except the weather.

But the letters Miss Frankie sends to my mama and me are

always full of things happening: Squeaky running off and never coming back, the movie house burning down, Arnold Cole being kicked by a mule, Uncle Virgil dying, and Aunt Mae going into the hospital and coming out again.

After dinner Jewel goes back to her shop, Daddy Lee takes his nap on the front room sofa, and JP is sent to his room to nap. I help Miss Frankie with the dishes, and when we finish, she says she could do with a nap herself, and couldn't I?

I go to my room, settle myself on the bed, and open the book my up-north grandmother gave me last Christmas, all about Joan of Arc and the Dauphin.

JP wakes me. He says we ought to go to town and help his mama.

Miss Frankie says, fine, but to be careful crossing the highway. At the highway, I take hold of JP's hand. We like to pretend the cars and semis are stampeded cattle. We look one way and then the other. When it is all clear, we run across.

First place we stop is the bank. We don't go in, just look through the window at JP's daddy, Charlie Henderson, who stands behind the counter and looks very important. His hair is slicked back and every day he wears a tie and a dress shirt.

When we get to Jewel's shop, there is only Doctor Hart's wife under the dryer. Her eyes are closed like she's asleep.

JP tells his mama, we come to help.

I always 'preciate that, Jewel says.

I get the broom and JP the dustpan. I sweep everything to one side in a pile and JP scoops it up. Then we run the back sink full of soapy water and shovel in this and that: combs, brushes, curlers, and whatnot.

Jewel sits down and begins fanning herself with a magazine. Her shop is hot when any of the dryers are on. After a bit, Jewel goes over and feels Mrs. Hart's head under the dryer. I think you're finished, she says, lifting the hood and propping it back.

Mrs. Hart gets up and toddles over to the chair in front of the mirror. Jewel helps her climb up and sit down, then she lifts off the hairnet. There are no pins or rollers, only long clips. Jewel takes these out and brushes Mrs. Hart's hair into a beautiful white waterfall.

Just like Jean Harlow, Jewel says, watching as Mrs. Hart disappears down the sidewalk.

Just like who? I ask.

An old-time movie star. We all do it, Jewel says. We fix on someone we'd like to be like. Ain't you Calamity Jane and isn't JP Matt Dillon?

Sometimes, I say, taking a hard look at Jewel. Here she has her own beauty shop but no curls in her own hair at all. She looks like pictures of Joan of Arc in my book.

Most of my ladies favor movie stars, Jewel says.

I had been thinking of asking Jewel to give me some curls, but I haven't seen enough movies to have a favorite movie star. So, who does Charlie Henderson think he is? I ask.

Durned if I know, she says.

What about Miss Frankie?

Lord, Etta, I didn't mean everybody.

It's the end of summer and I have to go back to Iowa. We wait on the platform, listening for the train. Tyler is the city of roses, Miss Frankie says, but the roses at the train station weren't as pretty as hers. Before the train comes, Daddy Lee gets some dirt in his eyes. He gives me a big hug, calls me his sugar-baby, then goes to sit in the pickup.

I wave from the train windows. The train passes through piney woods, around hills, across pastureland, and then through wheat fields shaved to the ground. Finally, there is nothing but chocolaty-brown dirt and the broken stalks where corn had been. This is Iowa. I wish I was not here.

My up-north Grandmother Lewis stays in bed, propped on pillows, except to go to the bathroom. All her breakfasts, dinners, and suppers are carried up to her room on a tray. Sometimes she asks me to rub her legs with a sweet-smelling lotion. Her legs are very white and soft, and if I poke them my fingerprints stay, like poking one of Miss Frankie's unbaked dinner rolls.

My mama tells me Grandmother Lewis's heart is too big and it makes her fill up with water. The doctors say that someday she will fill up with so much water she'll just drown on her own self.

Sundays, Father MacLaughlin comes. When I open the door, he rushes up the stairs without taking off his coat or his hat. He's carrying the Lord Jesus Christ under a big white handkerchief. He gives the Lord Jesus Christ to Grandmother Lewis, then comes back downstairs for a late breakfast. He says my mama makes the best biscuits in the whole wide world and him saying that makes her eyes sparkle. Then he goes back upstairs and stays with Grandmother Lewis until dinner time.

Mama explains that Father Mac, as she calls him, is like most preachers and doesn't have much money. She says he brings Grandmother Lewis solace, and we ought to be pleased to feed him as grandly as possible. He is a very skinny man.

When the next summer comes, I take the train with a note pinned to my collar. I have never learned to call up north home.

Summer is where home is, and JP and me coming to the supper table in our pajamas. Most days we manage to get so dirty that just face and hand washing won't do, so Jewel gives us a proper bath. She digs the washcloth into our ears and then scrubs the skin right off our necks.

My favorite supper is still raisin bran cereal with sweet milk and cinnamon toast, but Jewel is forever taking over the kitchen and making those fancy concoctions to smother left-over biscuits. The best is creamed tuna, the worst is chicken livers in a goopy sauce. She learns about these things from the ladies' magazines at her shop.

Once in a while after supper, JP's daddy comes calling with his tie sticking out of a pocket or hanging loose around his neck. He'll say howdy to me and JP and then we'll be put to bed, 'cause he really comes to see Jewel.

From behind the curtains in Jewel's front bedroom, me and JP peek out onto the porch without being seen. Sometimes Jewel sits with Charlie Henderson on the swing, but usually she perches herself on the porch rail.

He'll say: Thought maybe we could drive to Tyler Saturday night, take in a movie.

Thought maybe you'd come to see how JP's doing, she'll say. Maybe we can all go to the drive-in over in Jacksonville, he'll say. Maybe it's time you quit pestering me, she'll say.

On and on they go until we get tired of listening and go on to our rooms and to bed.

Chapter 9
Summering at the Lake

Another summer and for almost a month we all go to the lake cabin, all except Jewel who has to keep her shop open. She also keeps an eye on the garden in town, the watering and weeding, and the chickens, feeding them and gathering eggs. The big harvest will be at the end of summer, when Miss Frankie and Aunt Mae will do all the canning and freezing.

At the lake the first thing me and JP do is set about making ourselves a swimming hole between the boathouse and the pier. We clear the lakeweed by wading out and gathering it up on our legs, then walking it back to the shore and dumping it, then going back for more. When it's all clear, Daddy Lee brings in a pickup load of sand and shovels it out to cover the muddy lake bottom. Now we can see the bottom and make sure no snakes are hiding there. Daddy Lee dumps another load of sand out behind the cabin, making a sand pile for me and JP, then he hauls off the old lakeweed before it starts stinking.

The other side of the boathouse is already clear of lakeweed. A whole town of perch live there and raise their young'uns.

They build their homes by swishing their tails around and around, making little bowls in the mud bottom. It's a town of about a dozen little bowls.

After Squeaky ran off and never came back, Daddy Lee found himself a new dog. The new one is named Squeaky Two because she looks exactly like the old Squeaky, and she is just as good at getting snakes. We also have a gray cat that wandered up to the cabin and decided to stay. Miss Frankie calls him Puss, says he's a poor old thing someone forgot behind. Jewel calls him Devil, says nobody forgot him behind, that he was deliberately thrown away. Me and JP call him Smokey, and Daddy Lee doesn't call him anything. Squeaky Two mostly leaves him alone as she thinks he's meaner than any snake she's ever met.

Saw, saw, saw. Hammer, hammer, hammer. Daddy Lee makes noises that must carry clear across to the other side of the lake. First, he took out most of the wall between the front of the old cabin and the new part. Then he made a counter for eating at. On the kitchen side it has low stools, on the other side high ones because the added-on side of the cabin is two steps down from the old part.

Daddy Lee got the stools from Mr. Lightfoot at the Lone Star, broken stools from the backroom. He sawed the legs of some to fit the low side. The countertop is made from a skinny store-bought door, sanded clean and made shiny with three coats of varnish. Me and JP pay close attention to all of this.

The wood scraps from what Daddy Lee is doing gives us blocks to use in the town we are building in the sand pile out back. We smooth out roads and push the sand into hills outside of our town. We stand some of the wood scraps upright as storefronts, and some Daddy Lee nails one on top of another for us to use as cars and trucks. The smallest scraps we use as tombstones in the cemetery. Smokey supplies the dead bodies, mostly lizards.

One Saturday morning Jewel comes out in the Buick, hollering out the window and honking the horn as she drives up. For a surprise she has brought Aunt Mae and Uncle Luke and a cold watermelon. Right off, it is clear they are planning to stay over. Piled around Aunt Mae on the back seat are pillows and quilts. In the trunk is a half lug of peaches, that cold watermelon, and a sack of other stuff.

Daddy Lee cut down the weeds in front of the cabin when we first came. Now he and Jewel carry the kitchen table and chairs out under the sweetgum, and we all set to eating that watermelon while it's still cold. The grownups get the chairs, while Jewel, me, and JP sit on the ground. This is the first summer JP has learned to eat just the red part and spit out the seeds.

After the watermelon and some pimento cheese sandwiches Miss Frankie fixes, Daddy Lee and Uncle Luke go out fishing. Miss Frankie and Aunt Mae take an afternoon nap while me and JP splash around in our new swimming hole. Jewel who is set to watch us falls asleep in her sling chair.

We hear a commotion, Squeaky Two barking her head off. She wakes everyone up and brings me and JP running from the lake. She's out behind the cabin, way out back where the deep woods begin. We all arrive about the same time. Seems that Squeaky Two has cornered a varmint under the old outhouse.

Aunt Mae is afraid it is a snake, but Miss Frankie says it is probably just poor old Puss.

No way, Jewel says. That Devil would never let itself be cornered.

With no one watching or paying him attention, JP sneaks around the back side of the outhouse and crouches down. I see it, I see it, he yells.

Jewel and I run around and peek where JP is pointing.

A possum, Jewel says, and gathers Squeaky Two up in her arms. Leave it be, she says.

We all walk back to the cabin. I ask Miss Frankie if Squeaky Two would really kill the possum. Probably not, she says. Me and JP have not planned on burying anything quite so big in our cemetery.

Squeaky Two gets shut inside the cabin with us so the possum will have time to get away. Me and JP change into dry clothes, then we eat a peach and sit down at the new counter to play Seven-Up with Jewel. Miss Frankie and Aunt Mae set about turning most of that lug of peaches into pies.

We play the game real slow because JP has trouble holding so many cards at once. Squeaky Two whines around the back door. She is sure that possum is her business.

I saw your daddy the other day, Jewel says to JP. Can't say I ever saw him so liquored up.

Hush now, Jewel, Miss Frankie says. You've no call telling JP that.

I don't believe in keeping children ignorant, Jewel says.

No, you believe in giving them nightmares, Miss Frankie says, sounding put-out.

Jewel goes on in a la-la voice: I was reading just the other day about how having a sweet tooth is the same as being an alcoholic, that they're both just a sugar addiction.

You must read pure trash, Aunt Mae says, 'cause they ain't the same thing at all. Surely you know it was 'cause of drink that Luke lost his arm in that accident.

Why, I never knew Uncle Luke to drink, Jewel says, but you could tell she knew all about it.

Just you never mind, Aunt Mae says, 'cause he don't touch a drop no more.

I wonder what they would think about Grandmother Lewis keeping a bottle of Madeira and some pretty little glasses right on her vanity, right next to her fancy cut-glass perfume bottles and the picture of my daddy. How sometimes after Sunday dinner when Father Mac is there, and when she's had what she calls a good day, we all go up and have a little party with her.

My mama opens a window, and Father Mac sits next to it on a small fancy chair, crosses his legs, and lights a cigarette. Then they hold the little glasses, dainty-like, and talk about my daddy and things. Watching them in the big round vanity mirror is like watching people in a movie.

Daddy Lee and Uncle Luke come back grumpy from fishing. Everything they caught was too small and they had to throw 'em back. It doesn't matter as we have plenty of other stuff for supper. Plus, peach pie.

With the kitchen full of Miss Frankie and Aunt Mae, me and JP are not needed to help with the dishes. So, we help Daddy Lee bring out two cots from the back closet and set them up. Then we help Jewel fix sheets and blankets or quilts where everyone will sleep.

Miss Frankie and Aunt Mae will take the big bed, Jewel announces. Daddy Lee the top bunk, and you two (meaning me and JP) will share the bottom bunk. Uncle Luke and I will take the cots, because we're the skinniest.

But I want to sleep on a cot, I say.

Well, you can't, Jewel says.

How come you're so bossy? I ask. How come you always get to decide things?

That reminds me, Etta, she says. I don't want you bossing JP around. He gets quite enough of it from me. She reaches over and rumples his hair. Whadda you say, kiddo?

I give Jewel a hard look. It seems to me she's acting different than she used to, more wild like, almost as if she has a bit of the devil in her. I wonder where it was she saw Charlie Henderson liquored up 'cause he is never like that when he comes calling.

Once I asked my mama how come Aunt Mae and Uncle Luke never got married. She said she was only a child herself back then and had never learned the whole story, but it was complicated whatever it was. And when I asked her about Jewel being married to, but not living with Charlie Henderson, she said that was complicated, too.

When it comes time to go to bed, things don't go exactly as Jewel planned. Daddy Lee, even though he is not skinny, says he is taking one of the cots and Jewel can have the top bunk. So, we all settle in.

JP puts his head at one end of the bunk, and I put mine at the other. My feet in his face and his feet in mine. This does not suit JP at all.

You stink, he whispers.

I do not, I whisper back.

You two hush, Daddy Lee says.

I scrunch my legs up for a while but decide there is no way I can sleep like that all night. So, I turn around and put my head next to JP's

I don't wanna sleep with you, he whispers.

I put my fingers to his lips and whisper in his ear, soon as your mama's asleep, I'll help you climb up with her in the top bunk. She won't like that, he whispers back.

Again, I press his mouth with my fingers, and we wait. When

everyone's breathing is quiet and some are starting to snore, I help JP up to the top bunk and watch as Jewel wraps her arms around him.

Then I go over to Daddy Lee and shake him. Wake up, I whisper. JP is sleeping up with his mama. You can have the bottom bunk and I can sleep here.

It doesn't take any more persuading than that.

Chapter 10
Pups are Born

We are traveling in a spaceship, like Flash Gordon in the Sunday funnies. Packets of Kool-Aid with only a bit of sugar is our food for space travel, and the platform in the chinaberry tree is our spaceship.

Lick your finger first, I tell JP and hold out the packet of Kool-Aid. JP licks one finger, puts it into the packet, and then into his mouth. He makes a funny face at how sour it is.

A wasp comes buzzing at us and I swat at it, not enough to make it angry, but enough to make it go away. Wasps love chinaberry trees at the end of summer when the berries turn a mushy orange and start going rotten.

Though up in the chinaberry tree is my favorite place to be, spaceship is not my favorite let's pretend. I'm wishing for something more interesting to happen when I hear Miss Frankie calling us. We scramble down. We would not hurry so fast if she was calling us to come in, but it is much too early for that. We run to the outbuilding where Miss Frankie is waiting at the door.

Squeaky's having pups, she says. She means Squeaky Two.

Of course, me and JP knew it was coming. Anyone could see Squeaky Two's stomach was getting bigger and bigger, and it wasn't from eating too much. I put my hand out and JP takes it.

We step into the first room, the room with the deep freeze, full of summer's bounty as Miss Frankie calls it. On the other side is a row of bookcases with glass fronts, full of books from a great uncle on Miss Frankie's side, one I never knew. The room behind is long with three small windows on the back side covered over with newspapers so no one can peek in. Miss Frankie pulls the string for the overhead light, a small light for a big room.

Me and JP walk to where Squeaky Two is lying on a piece of old blanket stuffed into a cut-off box.

I don't see any pups, I say.

Soon, Miss Frankie says.

Me and JP sit on the floor next to the box, and when JP reaches out to pet Squeaky Two, she snaps at him.

Let her be, just watch, Miss Frankie says as she leaves us.

So, we settle back and watch Squeaky Two, watch her panting like from running on a hot, hot day, watch ripples run up and down her shiny black hair.

What's that? JP asks.

I lean closer to Squeaky Two, but I don't see anything.

No, JP says, over there.

He means something on the far side of the room, but there's such a conglomeration of things: harnesses hanging on the wall along with a couple of old gray uniforms, some saddles up on sawhorses, and branding irons leaning in a corner from when my daddy and Daddy Lee had some cattle, back when I was a baby. So, I wasn't exactly sure which of the things JP is asking about.

That, he says again, and I sight down his finger.

That's Daddy Lee's safe, I tell him.

JP scoots over to it and I follow. Is there gold in it? JP asks.

No, I tell him. That's where Daddy Lee keeps the deeds to his land and such.

Deeds? What's deeds?

Pieces of paper telling about Daddy Lee's land. Where it is, how big it is, stuff like that.

JP shakes his head. I bet there's gold in there, too.

Lord Almighty, I say. There ain't any gold. There's just those deeds and such like that.

Open it, JP says.

Cain't, I tell him.

He begins spinning the lock. Do it like at the post office, he says.

It's not the same and I don't know the numbers. I scoot back over to Squeaky Two and ignore JP.

The room is full of the smell of saddles and leather, reminding me of when I was really small, and my daddy would put me in front of him on a horse. I remember him holding on to me. I saw a photo of us on the horse, but I can't remember seeing any cattle. My mama told me about how after she and my daddy ran off up north and got married, and after I was born, they came back. My daddy wanted to be a cowboy. He and Daddy Lee got some cattle, but they all got sick and died. I sure wish those cows hadn't died, because then my daddy would not have been killed up north in that accident.

JP is still twirling numbers, so sure he can figure out how to open that safe, when Squeaky Two gives a small yelp, lifts her hind leg and something starts coming out of her.

I hiss at JP, quit worrying about that safe and get over here.

He doesn't even look around, just shakes his head. I almost got it, he says.

There's a pup coming out and you're acting like a dummy. I give him warning. If you don't get over here now, I'm gonna thrash you. And when he still doesn't let go of that safe, I go over and hit him. He swats back at me, and I grab his arm and start pulling, and then Miss Frankie is there yanking us apart and giving us what for. When we all go over to Squeaky Two, she's had two pups.

We watch as three more come out. In all she has five pups, every one black like her. They swarm around her middle. Their eyes are squinted shut like they're asleep and don't wanna wake up.

Aren't they cute, Miss Frankie says.

To me they look more like mice than dogs, and JP squeezes his eyes shut and copies their little whimpering noises.

Then Miss Frankie says it's time to get washed up for supper, but JP says he can't 'cause his mama's not home yet.

She'll be along directly; Miss Frankie tells him. Etta, here, can draw the water while I fix supper.

In the bathroom, JP perches himself on the closed commode and won't get undressed.

You know you have to, I tell him. We gotta check for ticks, I say, as I peel off my t-shirt, drop my shorts, and kick them aside. Come on, I say.

No, he says. Not 'fore my mama gets here.

I turn on the water taps and as the tub fills, I search my legs for ticks, and lift my arms to inspect all over. Come on, I say, dropping my panties. You know I cain't see my own back. I step backward toward JP. Well, I ask, do you see any?

You got a smelly butt, JP says.

I do not. I wipe myself, but you're such a baby you need your mama to help wipe your butt.

You made the water too hot, he says.

Did not. I made it just right. By then I've given up on JP. I'm standing in the tub, working up my nerve to sit down in the water that is a bit too hot. Here, I say, turning on the cold water, since you are such a baby.

Where's my mama?

Such a baby, I say again, and I take my whole bath while he pouts. I step out and I'm drying myself when Jewel bursts in the door. She looks like a wild woman, her face red and her neck all sweaty.

Squeaky Two had pups, JP says.

I know all about it, she says. Now you get your behind in that tub this instant. She goes straight to the sink and splashes her face with cold water.

Quick as I can I put on my pajamas, and when JP gets off the commode, I sit myself there. JP wiggles off his shorts, then Jewel squats down and yanks off his t-shirt with one quick jerk.

Ow, he cries, cupping his hands over his ears.

I'll give you ow's you won't never forget, she tells him. Now turn around so I can see if you got any ticks. You know we got to find them when they're small and not later when they're all fat and full of blood. After not finding any, she hurries him into the tub and sets to scrubbing him all over.

You smell funny, JP says, wrinkling his nose.

Why you little scamp, Jewel says, throwing down the wash rag and sitting back on her heels. Here I am slaving all day at that hot beauty shop, and then giving the place a good cleaning, and coming home feeling tired as all get-out, feeling like a wore-out rag doll. There's not one bone in my body that don't ache. Why I feel like I was shook silly and pushed up against one of those dirty walls and every inch of sweetness I'd been saving up was sucked right out of me.

Jewel started off angry, but by the end I think she's gonna cry. Me and JP don't say a word. We hardly dare breathe. Then Jewel helps JP from the tub and dries him off.

And tomorrow, she says, you won't be able to tell I cleaned a damned thing. Those darned windows are sitting all crooked and let in every speck of dirt that blows through this town.

She helps JP into his pajamas, then tells us to go on in to supper, so she can wash off that funny smell.

For supper Miss Frankie made cornbread sticks with stewed tomatoes and okra. Daddy Lee eats hot peppers with his. And then we have fresh blackberries from Uncle Luke's with a bit of cream and sugar.

Daddy Lee finishes first and goes to check on the new pups. Miss Frankie says she moved them from the back room to a corner of the washroom and left the door propped open so Squeaky Two can come and go.

Me and JP eat the berries as slow as we can, trying to make them last forever. From where I'm sitting, I can watch Jewel and Miss Frankie going about the kitchen business, washing and drying and putting away dishes. I hear Miss Frankie say Daddy Lee won't put up with something, but I can't hear what it is he won't put up with. And I see Miss Frankie touch Jewel's arm and Jewel start to push her hand away, then take hold of it.

What can we be tomorrow? JP wants to know.

Hush, I say. I'm trying to hear the kitchen business.

Then Jewel says something, but JP wrecks it by pushing his chair back and making a racket. I want to smack him.

First thing in the morning, me and JP go to see the pups. Jewel comes with us. She hasn't seen them yet.

What happened? JP cries.

Squeaky Two smiles up at us, but there are only two pups where there should be five.

A varmint musta got them, I say.

Jewel shakes her head. Miss Frankie did it. She drowned the others in a bucket.

Not Miss Frankie, I tell her. Miss Frankie said they're so cute.

Me and JP are all set to have a good cry, but Jewel gives us both a shake. Listen up, she says. These are not pets. These are working dogs. If Daddy Lee says to keep only two, you can be sure there's a good reason for it.

JP starts to cry anyway and goes running off to find Miss Frankie, never mind she was the one who did it.

So, how did she do it? I ask.

Lord, Etta. First, she got a bucket, then she put some water in it, and ...

No, I say. How did she know which ones to drown and which ones to keep?

Lord, Etta, Jewel says again as she leaves.

I take a good hard look at those two pups. It is a real puzzlement to me how Daddy Lee or Miss Frankie could tell which pups would make a good snake dog and which won't.

Chapter 11
Grandmother Lewis Passes

You can just take off that hangdog face, Jewel tells me. I turn away and look out the side window at the trees and fence posts flying by. We are on the way to Tyler for me to catch the train going north. Miss Frankie and JP are in the back seat. When I turn around to look, I see he's asleep with his head in her lap.

Jewel asks if I remember the time she helped me to stay. That was back then, she says. Now you don't got a choice.

I know that, I say. But I don't have to like it, do I?

That, she says, is entirely up to you. But I hope you don't act hangdog the whole time you're up north and make your mama miserable.

I shake my head. It's not that bad up there.

Then Jewel says the most surprising thing. She says she'd give anything to be in my shoes. She says the only way people ever get to go somewhere else is if they have no choice. Like boys going off to be soldiers or being run out of town for thieving or stuff like that.

Miss Frankie lifts her voice and says that's not quite right. She says the oldest Walker boy took himself off to college and never came back. Jewel says poo, says Henry Walker only went off to college so he wouldn't have to marry Sarah Vermillion.

Miss Frankie says sometimes that works the other way.

Tooshay, Jewel says, and starts telling us about an article she read about a certain Hollywood lady who had special surgery on her legs to make wearing high-heels feel natural. But what would happen if that poor Hollywood lady lost all her high-heeled shoes? Just imagine that lady waking up in her pink satin sheets, swinging her legs over the side of the bed, looking to slip her feet into her pink satin high-heeled mules with puff balls on the toes, and they're not there. Gone. Just disappeared. Why that poor lady would have to crawl across the room to the closet. Then, what if she finds all her high-heels shoes are gone.

Miss Frankie says that any Hollywood lady could ring the phone right by her bed, and the store would deliver however many new pairs of high-heeled shoes she wanted.

Oh, Miss Frankie, Jewel says, that's not the point.
Me and Miss Frankie never do learn exactly what was the point, because right then the Highway Patrol zips out from behind the big Tyler Chevrolet billboard, lights flashing, siren going loud enough to wake JP.

Jewel puts on a la-la voice and tries to sweet talk her way out, but she gets a ticket anyway. I hate Tyler Chevrolet, she says, handing the ticket back to JP for him to look at.

I'm thinking back to that day, as I watch out the front room window, kneeling on the sofa, holding the curtains apart only a little so as not to let the cold in, praying for the Buick to hurry because Grandmother Lewis is upstairs dying.

I think back to waiting for the train and walking around the platform on my tippy-toes, pretending I'm wearing high-heeled shoes and feeling a mean tightness all up the back of my legs. I could see the Buick sitting in the parking lot and thinking how much it looked like a big green toad. I pointed it out to JP who said I was crazy.

But I think the same thing again when I finally see, through the crack in the curtains, the Buick coming up the street, bringing Miss Frankie and Daddy Lee.

When I open the door, Miss Frankie gives me a hug and goes straight upstairs. Daddy Lee and I head for the kitchen and sit at the table. I make us a pot of tea. But he says he never takes his hot, so I cool his down and pour it over ice, even though it is cold enough outside to snow.

This is a dark house, he says.

I nod. It's true that most every room has dark paneling. I tell him I have to make sure I have a good light for reading, so I don't wreck my eyes. Father Mac says I read too much, says I should listen more to the radio.

Daddy Lee raises his eyebrows.

Father Mac says radio programs that make people laugh are good. He says they help people be happy and look at their problems with a different perspective.

Fancy word, Daddy Lee says.

I shrug and tell him I don't have any problems.

Daddy Lee looks up at the ceiling. I look up, too. We are both wondering how things are going up there.

Grandmother Lewis has been feeling poorly since Christmas, and she's been dying for the past week. Nothing the doctor says can make her go into the hospital. I never knew dying was so hard. I thought if you didn't get shot or killed right off, then you just close your eyes and never wake up.

I'm also wondering if Miss Frankie can do anything, but my

mama told me it just isn't possible in this situation. But mostly I'm hoping that when Grandmother Lewis dies, we will all get in the Buick and go home.

I make more tea. Daddy Lee and I sit and wait. Finally, Father Mac comes down the back stairs and says it is all over. He tells us he called the coroner from upstairs, as he goes over to the sink, parts the curtains above it, and looks out. He says he told them not to come for the body until morning. Miss Frankie ... is it okay I call her that? he asks, looking over his shoulder at Daddy Lee, who nods.

Miss Frankie's with Vesta, and I better get a move on before the snow gets any deeper. Then he shakes Daddy Lee's hand, gives me a hug, then rushes to get his overcoat and leaves.

Daddy Lee and I had been so busy doing nothing I hadn't noticed the stillness that comes with a snowfall. We go out onto the porch and watch it dance in the headlights of Father Mac's car going down the street.

I hadn't realized y'all's preacher is such a young man, Daddy Lee says.

I shake my head. He's Grandmother Lewis's preacher. He says my mama is a very stubborn woman.

Yes, Daddy Lee says, your mama's always been that way.

When Miss Frankie comes down, she says she'll take us upstairs. She says my mama is sleeping, and Daddy Lee said he'd just as soon not see the body but would take their suitcase up to where they'd be sleeping. The house is a big one with five bedrooms, so Daddy Lee follows me and Miss Frankie up the main stairs and I show him which one is theirs.

Then Miss Frankie and I go to Grandmother Lewis's room. She's lying down flat on the bed, not propped up as she likes to be. I go and sit down on the bed next to her and touch her hand. She's cold, I say.

Yes, Miss Frankie says. We left the window open on purpose, so she'll stay cold till they come get her tomorrow.

She looks real peaceful, I say.

Poor woman, Miss Frankie says, she wanted to leave so bad. That young preacher mumbling his prayers, he finally gave up trying to get her to pray along with him. She wouldn't have none of that. All she did was keep calling your daddy's name.

Guess she's with him now, I say, looking over at his picture on her vanity.

Miss Frankie nods. At the end, she was so quiet I wasn't exactly sure when she left. Sometimes folks aren't quite ready, and they get confused at being dead. They kinda hang around, maybe not knowing they are really dead or not knowing where to go. But your grandmother was ready, Etta. She's gone.

Early the next morning I hear fussing in the kitchen. I stop at the top of the backstairs and listen, but it's only Daddy Lee and Miss Frankie talking. I turn and go down the hallway to my mama's room.

I knock and go on in. She says she's glad to see me, and she hurries to get up and dress. I hope you weren't scared last night, she says, the body still being here and all.

No, I say, and tell her Miss Frankie said Grandmother Lewis wasn't spooking around here like a haunt, that she was already in heaven with my daddy.

My mama nods and says Miss Frankie was able to soothe Grandmother Lewis, to get her to relax and breathe slowly. But her calling your daddy's name over and over made me miss him so much. I must'a cried half the night. Then I slept, slept real hard.

I watch as she tidies the room and makes her bed. Now come

here, she says. We sit side by side on her bed and she puts her arms around me, hugs me tight. Did you have a good cry? she asks.

Not yet, I say.

That morning I can hear how my mama's voice has changed back to how it used to be, soft sounding like Miss Frankie's. Never mind the elocution lessons my mama took so she'd sound more up-north. And now she's taking singing lessons. She always goes down to the basement, around behind the big furnace, to practice her la-la-la's so as not to disturb Grandmother Lewis. I guess now she's gonna do her la-la-la's upstairs.

I do cry a little bit at the funeral. Other people are crying, and the snow on the ground at the cemetery is so bright it's enough to make anyone's eyes water. But I really cry when we get home, up in my own room and into my pillow. I cry because Daddy Lee and Miss Frankie are going back home, and they aren't taking us with them.

Father Mac has a plan for my mama to take in college student boarders and for her to go to college herself. It is not a plan I am pleased with at all but when I try talking to my mama about it, she's busy writing notes to a bunch of Grandmother Lewis's relatives. All those relatives are far-away, Christmas-card relatives, mama calls them, and they have to be told in writing, not by telephone.

You could go to beauty school like Aunt Jewel did and then work with her in her beauty shop, I say.

My mama snorts at that. What, two beauty operators in a one-dog town? And she goes on with her note writing.

I remember that Highway Patrolman saying for a little lady, Jewel sure has a heavy foot, and Father Mac saying my mama is a very stubborn woman, and more than once hearing Daddy Lee muttering about those headstrong gals, so I know better than to waste any time telling my mama that I personally know a huge number of dogs in that town.

Chapter 12
At the Lake, Berry Picking

For three summers my mama makes up reasons I can't go home to visit. Finally, she says my moping around is driving her crazy. It helps that our boarders, Carmen and Mark, tell her they can't stand looking at me being so miserable.

Now I kneel at the edge of the pier and look down at the shadow my face makes in the water. I watch minnows cross from one cheek to the other, then dart away. Lakeweed and the murkiness of the water hide the bottom. This year me and JP did not clear a place for swimming. Seems neither one of us is interested.

I scoot back and roll over, feeling the splintery wood beneath the towel. I put an arm over my eyes against the brightness. A small lake breeze cools me. Then the pier shakes from footsteps. I sit up.

Jewel stops at the edge of my towel. I see you're getting yourself some bosom, she says.

I look down at the small plumpness under the stretchy material of my bathing suit. Most people comment on how I've grown, but they mean how tall I'm getting. It is just like Jewel to mention bosoms instead.

Anyway, Jewel tells me, Miss Frankie says for you to get out of the sun, that you've had enough for one day.

I pick up the towel and head toward the cabin, turning once to scan the lake for Daddy Lee and JP who went out fishing. Instead of following Jewel inside, I walk around to the back of the cabin where me and JP had once played hour after hour. Our old sandpile is mostly covered over with weeds and pine straw and way out back where the deep woods begins is a pile of rotting wood where the outhouse used to be. When I look back to the cabin, I can see the different colored roof shingles and understand how small it used to be before Daddy Lee added on to it.

I go and change into shorts and a t-shirt. Jewel is sitting at the counter playing solitaire, and Miss Frankie is in the rocking chair by the open front door. There's a book on her lap, but she spends as much time looking out at the lake as she does at her book.

Sit down, Jewel tells me. I don't want you watching. I can only win this if I cheat, and I don't want any witnesses.

So, I go around to where the bunks are, where our things are packed to go back into town. I get the drawing tablet Carmen gave me. Carmen's studying to be a real artist.

I settle myself at the far end of the counter, away from Jewel and her cheating, and with my back to the lake, leaving Miss Frankie to watch for the boat. I draw a floor plan of how this lake cabin used to be.

I sure wish your mama would come down one of these summers, Miss Frankie says, without looking around at me. Her eyes are only for watching the lake.

Yes, ma'am, I say, but mama says she won't ever finish school if she doesn't take summer school. Mark and Carmen, they're both doing summer school, too.

After drawing the floor plan of how the lake cabin used to be, I add on what Daddy Lee added on. I know Carmen had meant for me to teach myself how to make real pictures, but I don't even feel like trying.

Jewel scrambles the cards together, then shuffles them for a new game. She spends as much time looking at the lake as she does at the cards she lays down. My patience is about wore out, she says, and if they don't hurry up and get back these cards are gonna be wore out, too.

What if something happened, I say. What if the boat turned over?

Hush, Etta, Miss Frankie says.

I hush and we wait.

Finally, in the late afternoon they come back with lots and lots of beautiful perch, and JP's face all sunburned as he wasn't wearing a hat. They gut and scale the fish, then pack them in the trunk of the Buick, all ready for the freezer. Some we'll have for supper tonight.

JP sits in the back between me and Jewel. He falls asleep right away, like he always does riding in the Buick. His head lolls between mine and Jewel's shoulders because the road is full of curves and the up and down of small hills. I can smell on him the lake and the fish they caught.

In town JP runs with a gang of boys. They all have BB guns and shoot at birds and tin cans. JP comes home later than we were ever allowed. Daddy Lee still takes his walks to the post office. Sometimes I go with him, but mostly I spend the days helping Miss Frankie in the garden and fixing meals or helping Jewel in her beauty shop.

One day in mid-summer, Jewel closes her shop early and

we take Daddy Lee's pickup to go berry picking. The bushes at Uncle Luke's have already been picked clean and put up by Aunt Mae and Miss Frankie. Jewel drives and we all squeeze into the cab, me in the middle. Miss Frankie hangs onto the door handle because Jewel, as always, is driving much too fast. Finally, Miss Frankie says, whoa, there, sister.

I had volunteered to sit in the back, but Miss Frankie said it warn't proper for young ladies to ride in the back of pickups. I am getting sick of all this young lady business when it means I can't run around barefoot, and JP treats me like I have cooties.

After a number of miles on the highway, Miss Frankie has Jewel turn down a narrow, paved road that passes farmhouses and fields of sweet potato vines. Then onto a single track of red dirt with a grass strip down the middle. There are no more planted fields, only small empty ones between wild thickets of trees and scrub.

Without being told, Jewel stops beside a driveway strung across with barbed wire, a driveway that leads to a house with boarded over windows. Behind it, the barn and outbuildings lean this way and that, all but ready to tumble down. Everything is gray as ashes except for the umbrella of a chinaberry tree and some pale magenta petunias gone wild beside the porch steps.

Miss Frankie tells me it's Daddy Lee's old family place, then tells Jewel to drive on, and Jewel drives us deeper into the woods. Finally, Miss Frankie points and says, There! The road looks more like a deer path through the woods, but Jewel puts the pickup down it, the scrub scratching both sides. At the end is a clearing and the ruins of a small house.

Jewel slams out of the pickup and goes off to find the berry bushes. Miss Frankie and I walk over to the old house, and she tells me this is where she was born.

Way out here? I say.

She tells me it was common in those days for people to live way out in the woods. She explains how in winter her daddy did some trapping and her mama kept a year 'round garden as winter is a good time for greens, turnips, beets, and such. She says when she and Luke were old enough to go to school, the family moved into town and her daddy went to work at the sawmill.

I follow her up to the door and she lifts the latch. Inside the floors and walls are naked wood. I see Miss Frankie smiling as if she has happy memories of living way out here.

We are back outside and walking around and Miss Frankie's telling me more about what it was like to live out here, when Jewel comes flouncing back, declaring those berries aren't worth picking. Never seen such puny things, she says.

But Miss Frankie says she remembers the berries on those bushes being extra sweet, so we each pick at least half a bucket.

Later I draw the floor plan of how I imagined that house had been. From the parts Miss Frankie showed me, I figure there had been only four rooms and a wide porch along the south side. JP comes in while I'm drawing and asks what it is I'm doing. I tell him.

What for? he asks.

I explain that it's like playing, like when we were little and used to make cities in the sand pile. He asks if he can do it too, so I give him some pages from my tablet. When he says he isn't interested in drawing floors of houses, I tell him to draw whatever he wants. He draws airplanes and soldiers and bombs exploding.

My daddy's in the war, he says.

He is not in any war, but I don't bother to say that to JP. Charlie Henderson is in Houston doing his yearly duty for the National Guard. There had been a letter from him early in the week and Jewel read parts of it at the table after supper, about him visiting the beach in Galveston.

Jewel saves any letters she gets in the back of her underwear drawer. I know this because every year I make a regular inspection of the whole place soon as I arrive. This year there are new curtains for the kitchen and pantry windows, a stuffed ottoman in the living room, and in the medicine cabinet is a fresh tin of black drawing salve, meaning JP must be having boils again.

And then there are the things people have left behind that tell me who has been to visit, like a paperback of the kind Uncle Walt likes to read, and one of Aunt Bessie's hair rats behind the black velvet hat that Cousin Valentine wears to funerals. Every year that hat is still on the chifforobe shelf, and every year I try it on, pulling the face veil down and cupping it under my chin.

Chapter 13
Daddy Lee's Fish Pond

The air is thick with dragonflies, more than I have ever seen in my life, all jitterbugging around the cattails at Daddy Lee's fish pond. As I watch them, I'm also listening to what Aunt Bessie is saying about my mama, about how my mama had forsaken her own kin to care for her mother-in-law, and how it reminds Aunt Bessie of the Book of Ruth. Them both being widows, she says.

You mean all four of them being widows, Jewel says.

Well, yes. Of course. But I meant Ruth and Vesta, and that Vesta reminds me of Ruth.

Bessie, Uncle Lum calls, bring me that other jug. Uncle Lum is one of Daddy Lee's brothers. His real name is John Columbus.

Widows, my foot, Jewel says when Aunt Bessie trots out of hearing range. Bessie was just warming up to dig at me with some Bible quote.

We're at the spring that feeds Daddy Lee's own personal fish pond. What was once a narrow hollow where he had a dam built across the far end, making a small lake hardly big enough to float a boat on. Sometimes when Daddy Lee goes fishing other places and catches fish too small to eat, he brings them here to live and grow bigger.

When I ask Jewel why he built it, she says building things is just something humans like to do. They like moving dirt from one place to another.

Like when me and JP used to build towns in the sand pile? Jewel nods. Exactly like that.

Critters do it too, I say. Wasps and dirt daubers build themselves houses. And the mama perch on the other side of Daddy Lee's boathouse build those little bowls to raise their young'uns in.

Goodness, Jewel says. I never thought about that. But they build only what they need. Do us humans need big cities?

We both sit quiet for a while and ponder.

I do wonder, Jewel says, how Uncle Lum manages to mix his whiskey drinking with Aunt Bessie's Bible thumping.

Uncle Lum and Aunt Bessie had stopped in at the house on their way back to Dallas from visiting some of Bessie's folks. They brought jugs to fill with good spring water. According to Uncle Lum, Dallas tap water ain't fit to mix with good whiskey, so they always want to fill up at Daddy Lee's spring that's off the back road to Palestine.

The cattails around the lake remind me of Aunt Bessie's rats, them being about the same size. How come she puts those rats in her hair? I ask Jewel.

For volume, Jewel says, and she explains how it works, how you fluff up a lady's hair by making it tangled. It's called ratting it, she says. Then you pin on the rats where you want more volume and smooth the ratted hair over and pin it down. Bessie's worn her hair like that for as long as I can remember, Jewel says. I must admit, she adds, it's not entirely unbecoming on her.

I remember watching at night how Aunt Bessie combs out her hair and gives it a lot of brushing, I say, and then she puts it in a long braid.

Men like that, Jewel says. I mean, I've read that men like women to have long romantic-looking hair.

You gonna grow yours long? I ask.

Don't think so, she says, but she puts her head to one side and stares off into nowhere like she might be thinking about it.

After the jugs are filled and loaded in the trunk, Aunt Bessie says she would sure like a fresh field melon to take back. So, Daddy Lee shows Uncle Lum the way to get out to the melon field next to Cole's.

The shade under the mulberry trees around Daddy Lee's spring had been cool and the breeze blowing in the car windows made the summer heat tolerable. The mid-day heat in the melon field is completely unbearable. Aunt Bessie says the dirt in the field looks a bit loose and since she has weak ankles she better wait in the car. Uncle Lum says something I can't hear, and he stays in the car too. They leave the car doors open, hoping to invite in a breeze, even a small one.

Jewel and I follow Daddy Lee into the field.

I ask Jewel why can't we just buy them a melon at one of the roadside stands. Jewel turns her mouth down, shakes her head, but doesn't say anything. She's holding a highway map over her head to keep the sun off.

I thought Daddy Lee would choose any old melon near where Uncle Lum had parked, but he keeps going farther and farther into the field, prying up melons and inspecting the undersides. Sometimes he bends over and gives one a knuckle thump.

Just as Aunt Bessie said, the dirt in the field is loose, and burning hot when it comes sliding into my sandals. I can see that Jewel is having the same trouble, and we both sorta stop following Daddy Lee and edge our way toward the bushes and trees between the field and Cole's house. We stand there in the shade and watch Daddy Lee, waiting for him to decide which melon.

We could be home drinking sweet tea, Jewel says. This must be God's punishment for something.

For not staying home and helping Miss Frankie with dinner, I say.

Daddy Lee's just showing off, Jewel says, all because of Uncle Lum being a city fella.

When Daddy Lee waves to us, we wade back through the hot dirt. He's picked out a melon and has crushed another one open by stomping on it. There is something awful about all the red spilling out into the dirt and about Daddy Lee's chin and hand dripping with melon juice. Have some, he tells us.

Jewel bends down and takes a handful. She leans over as far as she can so as not to drip juice on her blouse.

Have some, Etta, Daddy Lee says, and as I reach down, my eye catches a movement in the bushes. It must be one of Cole's boys spying on us.

I straighten up. But Daddy Lee, I say, these aren't our melons and somebody's over there watching us.

Daddy Lee turns to where I'm looking. Hey, Arnold, he calls and gives a beckoning wave. Come on over here.

I remember Miss Frankie writing to us that Arnold had been kicked by a mule, and when he gets closer, I can see something is not quite right. He looks normal enough, but the way he moves his head reminds me of Aunt Bessie trying to sight proper through her bifocals.

Give me a hand here, Daddy Lee says, and Arnold snaps the melon loose, picks it up, and walks ahead of us to the car.

He can't hear, Jewel says to me.

Sure, he can. He did just what Daddy Lee said.

No, he figured out what he was supposed to do, she says.

When we get to the car, Aunt Bessie is talking a blue streak to Arnold, but like Jewel said, he isn't hearing a word of it. Daddy Lee opens the trunk and Arnold puts the melon in, turns around, and walks off.

He quit talking too, Jewel says.

Because they have a long drive ahead, Aunt Bessie and Uncle Lum leave right after dinner. Jewel goes to her shop, Daddy Lee takes his nap, and JP sneaks off to be with his friends.

I help Miss Frankie with the dishes. She keeps handing me back plates with bitty spots on them to rewash. I don't believe all those spots are real, that some are really flaws in the china pattern. But I do as Miss Frankie says.

How come Daddy Lee can take whatever he wants from Cole's fields? I ask Miss Frankie.

Because it's his land and it's part of the arrangement, she answers.

Doesn't seem fair, I say.

If there's one thing he is, it's fair, so I don't wanna hear that kind of talk.

So, I talk about something else. I tell her I've been looking at how the floors in this house are different, like how the back room is stepped down from the rest.

Miss Frankie tells me that when Daddy Lee first built this house for him and Rosetta, the back room was a big back porch.

Did you know her? Rosetta?

Town this size ever'one knows ever'body. After Rosetta died, the whole town figured he and your Aunt Mae would get married, it being usual for a widower to marry one of his wife's unmarried sisters, and your Aunt Mae being Rosetta's only sister. But my brother Luke had been courting your Aunt Mae. Your mama and Jewel being such bitty things, Daddy Lee needed a new mama for them quickly.

So instead, you and Daddy Lee got married. How come Aunt Mae and Uncle Luke never got married?

I thought they would. Ever'one thought they would. Then he had his accident at the sawmill and lost his arm.

When the dishes are finished, Miss Frankie hangs the dish towel to dry on the oven door. I wait for her to say more.

It was this way, she says. Your Uncle Luke got it into his head that being married to a one-armed man would mean Aunt Mae wouldn't be taken care of properly. Sometimes I think he is too stubborn for his own good.

Instead of taking naps we went and sat at the table in the back room. I bring out my drawing tablet and Miss Frankie lays out some patterns and begins cutting quilt pieces.

So, what about Jewel and Charlie Henderson? I ask.

Miss Frankie shakes her head. Neither your mama nor Jewel ever did a thing they didn't want to do, she says. Lee spoiled them. Those girls never learned to make do.

Somehow that doesn't seem true. Way I see it, both Jewel and my mama are making do.

I open my tablet to the page with the house in the woods, and Miss Frankie points out to me where I put the chimney wrong. It was in between the parlor and the kitchen, she says. That way it could be used from both sides. Before we got a real stove, we cooked in the fireplace. The parlor, she tells me, was for formal visits and the laying out of coffins. Her folks were poor so there had not been a lick of furniture in her mama's parlor, just straight-backed chairs brought in from the kitchen and porch when strangers or death came calling.

Chapter 14
Driving, Storm Cellar Bet

Every afternoon Miss Frankie turns on the floor fans. They make a loud purring sound that will put anyone to sleep. Outside, the leaves of the trees and bushes droop in the heat, but the air is always cooler under the mimosa where Daddy Lee parks the pickup. When we were younger, me and JP liked to sneak away from our naps to play in the pickup, pretending it was an aeroplane and we'd take turns being the pilot.

Today, I'm slouched in the front seat, my feet up on the dashboard, making my lap perfect to hold the magazine I filched from Jewel's shop. With both doors open a small breeze comes through and lifts the magazine pages. I'm reading a story about a woman whose husband ran off and then comes back and how she is planning to get her revenge. As Aunt Mae would say, it is pure trash.

I close my eyes and imagine myself with a husband. I make him look a little like Father Mac, but of course not a priest. And to get revenge, I rub his toothbrush across a bar of soap.

My mama always says it's okay to read anything as long as it makes you think. Besides her schoolbooks, she reads books for her ladies' club. She tried to get our boarder Carmen to join, but Carmen says a group of only ladies can only be extremely boring.

I imagine Mark, our other boarder, as a husband, but there is no way I could play dirty tricks on him. Mark is quiet and shy and studying to be a doctor. I have never known anyone to study as hard as he does. Carmen says she thinks he is a weird bird. My mama thinks Carmen is sweet on him. My school friends who've seen him say he's good looking, and he is, in a pale sort of way.

My mama once told me Mark was raised in an orphanage and was adopted when he was about six years old by a widow-lady whose husband had owned a paper mill. The widow-lady didn't have any children of her own, so when she died, Mark didn't have any family at all.

I'm thinking how awful it would be to have no family at all when I hear the creak of the screen door. I look over and see it's Daddy Lee who's sneaked away from his naptime.

Hey, I call, not too loud, and he comes over. He now has a cane from when he hurt his leg out hunting. He tripped over a dog, and it made him so mad he got rid of all his hounds, just sold them away.

He asks what I'm doing and I tell him I'm not doing anything. He says we should go for a ride. He says by my age both my mama and Jewel knew how to drive and he will show me how.

He gets in the passenger side and has me scooch as close to the steering wheel as possible. By stretching my legs as long as I can, my foot reaches the pedals. To see out the front window, I have to look under the top of the steering wheel.

Then he tells me which pedal is for what. I touch each one with my foot and repeat over and over which is which: clutch, brake, gas, clutch, brake, gas.

Fine, he says. Now we'll do this real quiet. He shows me how to undo the parking brake and the pickup begins rolling back into the street. He reaches over and swings the steering wheel hard one way and then the other until we are rolling front ways down the street past the Halbert's.

You just mind the pedals and the steering, he says, and I'll do the shifting. When we begin to pick up speed, he turns the key and tells me to put the clutch all the way in and then, when he tells me, I'm to let my foot off real fast and give it some gas. He wiggles the gear shift and then yells, Now! I let my foot off the clutch as quick as I can. The pickup gives a pop, like a gun going off. Daddy Lee reminds me to give it some gas, and when I do the engine roars, and we are riding along as though driving is something I always knew how to do.

The Mosley's fence at the end of the road comes up quicker than I expect. Daddy Lee tells me to take my foot off the gas and press on the brake. Then he pulls the wheel his way at the end of the fence. The pickup skids around the turn. When I put my foot back on the gas, like he tells me, we are just fine.

We're on the back road to Tyler and for a while there are no hills or curves. He tells me hardly anyone uses this road any more as the new highway is shorter and faster.

How'm I doing, I ask, mostly just to see if I can drive and talk at the same time.

Fine, he says, you're doing just fine.

Kinda poky, though.

No, he says. You don't need to be a speed demon like Jewel.

After a while and before we reach the Neches Bridge, he tells me to take my foot off the gas, to push a bit on the brake, and to push the clutch all the way in. He jiggles the gear shift. I push more on the brake and the pickup rolls slowly off the road. He turns off the key and helps me set the parking brake. Then he tells me about the plans to dam the Neches, like at the fishing lake and his little lake. But, he says, this would be a lake hundreds of times bigger than any lake around here.

I'm reminded of Jewel and me pondering over human beings building things, more and bigger things than they need. Then Daddy Lee says that such a big lake would be a reservoir, a place to hold water needed in nearby towns and cities.

Come this fall and God willing, he says, while rubbing his bad knee, I'll be able to walk the area and see how much lumber there is worth saving.

I knew from the fishing lake that some trees must be left to hold the land in place, so it won't all slide down to the bottom and make just a big mud hole.

First thing when we get back, I trot into the house and announce that I know how to drive. Jewel is at her beauty shop, but Miss Frankie is properly impressed, and I set out to find JP. This summer he is especially thick with Tom Simms and Billy Daniels and their favorite hangout is the farthest pear tree in the way back of the Vermillion's next door. That particular tree is an old fire-blighted thing that never gives fruit anymore.

Only I don't have to go that far. I find JP near the butane tank looking down into the opened door of the storm cellar. When we were small, we pretended the dirt-covered top was an Indian burial mound because that's what it looks like.

I crouch down beside JP and look down the brick steps that lead to a floor covered with damp leaves. I imagine a ceiling of spider webs. I have never known the cellar to be used to hide from tornados, though surely it has been.

JP tells me Tom and Billy bet him he can't stay down there a whole night. From the worried look on his face, it is easy to tell who's gonna win that bet.

You oughtn't to have let yourself be tricked into making that kind of bet, I say.

You're a girl and you don't know nothin', he says.

And you're a fool, I say. Only way you're gonna stay down there is standing up all night long. You're crazy if you think Miss Frankie's gonna let you take a good pallet or a good quilt down in that dirty place when there's no storm to be hiding from.

Fool, I say again. And I remember Miss Frankie saying three little boys being best friends is asking for trouble. They get wore out playing and two of them turn on the other.

You ought to get Tom and Billy to stay down there, too, I say. It's only fair.

You don't know nothin', he says again.

That is when I tell him that on the contrary, I do know something, that I know how to drive. And that I know all about a new lake that's gonna be built.

I don't know how I let JP trick me, but when we are sure everyone is asleep, we get a pair of camp stools from the pantry and sneak out through the side door. The Vermillion's dog sets to barking but shuts up when she figures it's just us. I hold the flashlight and JP carries the camp stools down the steps. Under our pajamas we have on real clothes.

You know it won't count if they find out you stayed with me, he whispers.

Listen, I whisper back, I promised, and I still promise, cross my heart a million times.

You sure?

Lord almighty, JP, I'm sure.

I decide talking in a normal voice might make it seem like we are sitting in a regular little room instead of where we really are.

So, JP, I say, what is it you gonna be when you grow up?

JP is holding the flashlight and I see him shrug. I'm gonna be a soldier like my daddy, he says.

Your daddy isn't a real soldier, I say. He works at the bank. I suppose you could join the National Guard like he did.

I suppose, he says, handing me the flashlight and suddenly not seeming in the talking mood.

Me, I think about Daddy Lee and what he said about the new lake, about how it might bring all kinds of possibilities and new jobs. I think about being a farmer, but I don't really know a thing about farming. I think about working in a beauty shop. I think about my mama going to college. I seem to be doing more thinking than my brain can hold.

JP is falling asleep. I figure as soon as he falls off the stool, I can talk him into going back inside to bed and then flat-out lying to Tom and Billy. How are they to know any different?

While I wait, I shine the light around. The walls and ceiling are not full of spider webs. If me and JP were just little furry animals, we could curl up together in a corner and go to sleep.

Chapter 15
Mrs. Cole Rids Herself

Miss Frankie and Aunt Mae set off early for Jacksonville to shop for things like coffee, sugar, flour, cornmeal, and whatever else is needed for the next month. Daddy Lee's gone fishing with JP, this time to his favorite spot underneath the old Neches bridge which will disappear when the new lake fills. Daddy Lee's leg is much better, and he has no problem driving the pickup on the back roads. If he goes slowly, he says.

Daddy Lee and JP aren't expected back until late afternoon. My drawings are spread out on the big table. I think about drawing a house I have never seen before, a house made up of parts I like from real houses I know. But first, I need to think up someone to make it for, think up who is gonna live in it.

Jewel hasn't gone anywhere. I can hear her sweeping the floor of the back room, then the creak of the screen door and her sweeping the back steps.

As I sit thinking, I watch the patch of sunlight on the floor beside the French doors get smaller and smaller as the sun inches its way toward noon. Across from me in the front room is the sofa where Daddy Lee takes his afternoon naps under his newspaper tent, looking as if he was laid out, looking as if death had come calling.

Since Jewel is determined to never live with Charlie Henderson again, I decide to make a house for Carmen and Mark, my mama's boarders, as if they've gotten married. But before I can make a single line on the paper, Jewel flounces into the room. She stops, looks over my shoulder at the blank paper, then goes over and sits on the piano stool.

Why do we have that old piano? I ask. Nobody ever plays it. Jewel twirls around, opens the piano lid, and plunks out a few notes. My mama knew how, she says. Daddy Lee probably bought this for her. And your mama knows how, and so does Aunt Mae.

I've never seen Aunt Mae play, I say.

Jewel tells me Aunt Mae and Uncle Luke were once quite a pair, even after his accident. She tells me Uncle Luke played with the bow tied to his coat sleeve where his arm ended. It's complicated, Jewel says. Then she shows how, pretending to hold a fiddle under her chin and bending her other arm like it's broken and has a bow tied to it. Her bent arm looks like how Miss Frankie tucks a chicken's wings before roasting a whole bird.

Does he ever still play the fiddle? I ask.

Jewel shakes her head.

Then she shows me a song on the piano. She sings, a word for each note she plays, heart-and-soul-I-fell-in-love-with-you-heart-and-soul-the-way-a-fool-would-do-mad-ly-with-all-my-heart-and-soul, over and over until I have it memorized. I stand on the right side and plunk the high notes while she plays the middle with both hands. We play and sing it through perfectly twice, then she slams the lid down, twirls around on the piano stool, grabs me tight, and sings: madly with all my heart and soul.

What if, I whisper, you knew Charlie Henderson was dying?

Would you go and be married to him again?

But I don't know that, she says. I don't know that at all.

But what if?

Good Lord, Etta, she says, shaking her head.

We hear the sound of the Buick pulling into the carport and go to help carry groceries. Miss Frankie's Little Maid begonias in the flowerbed at the end of the carport are huddled under a coat of dust from Jewel's earlier sweeping. It's a small, round bed and I've been told that underneath is the old well, sealed over when the house got piped-in water.

Aunt Mae is still sitting in the Buick, looking through her pocketbook. Miss Frankie has walked out to the driveway and is reaching her arms to the sky, stretching out the tiredness from driving to Jacksonville and back.

Instead of fixing a real dinner, Jewel reheats a mess of peas and greens, and Miss Frankie makes a quick pan of cornbread and slices some cantaloupe. Daddy Lee and JP aren't expected back until near suppertime.

Instead of napping, Miss Frankie drives Aunt Mae home and leaves Jewel at her beauty shop where she has to give Mrs. Briggs a permanent wave. While she's gone, I wash the dishes, clean the kitchen, and put the groceries away.

When she gets back, I tell her to go on and take a nap.

Not today, she says. I need to check on Linda Cole. You can come with me if you want. I would appreciate your help getting things together to take to her.

She sets me to making a batch of ice box cookies from rolls already in the ice box. I pull out the rolls and set to slicing them. I see Miss Frankie watching me. You're looking at me funny, I say. Am I doing this wrong?

Miss Frankie shakes her head. No, Etta, I was just thinking how much you remind me of your daddy, your lips pooched out just like him when he was concentrating real hard.

He must have been really something, the way you and Jewel and my mama go on and on about him.

I place the slices on a sheet pan and sprinkle them with sugar, then shove the pan in the oven that's already been heated.

Miss Frankie finishes taking chicken pieces out of the fry pan. While the cookies bake, I help her cover the platter of chicken and put it into a cardboard box along with some store-bought bread, some bologna, a jar of mayonnaise, the rest of the pan of cornbread we had earlier, a jar of her butter pickles, and a jar of her very special fig preserves.

We save out some chicken for Daddy Lee and JP to eat when they return, to tide them over before supper.

When the cookies are finished, and have cooled a bit, we add them to the box. I help Miss Frankie carry it out and put it in the Buick's trunk. Then we drive to Cole's. Miss Frankie tells me she heard Linda Cole is laid up with some female trouble.

Cole's place seems deserted. Now that Daddy Lee no longer keeps a pack of hunting dogs, the only sound comes from some young roosters practicing their crowing. I suppose Mr. Cole and the boys must be out in the fields.

Miss Frankie knocks softly and then we let ourselves in. We find Mrs. Cole in bed under a pile of rumpled quilts. Her face has no color and I'm afraid she's dead. But when Miss Frankie calls her name, she opens her eyes.

Soon as she sees us, she groans and turns her face to the wall. I be such a mess, she whispers.

Miss Frankie tells her everything is going to be fine, and then tells me to go put the groceries away and put a big pot of water on the stove to heat.

In the kitchen I find every surface covered with dirty plates, pots, and pans, while a swarm of flies feasts on the overflowing slop bucket. The rest of the house is tolerably clean and only in need of a good sweeping and mopping.

The groceries are on the porch, the box too heavy for me to carry alone. I clear the kitchen table and carry the things in one by one. Before setting to washing everything, I carry the slop bucket out and dump it over the chicken yard fence. The flock fights over those scraps like they haven't been fed in a week.

I rinse the slop bucket under the outdoor faucet. The air is full of the icy scent of mint from a patch growing around the flat stone where the faucet drips.

Back inside, I clear the sink so I can fit a big pot under the spigot and then clear the stove top of dirty pots and pans to make room to heat the big one. I then turn back to the sink. There's only cold water and bar soap, but I make do. I stack the washed dishes on one side of the drain board. When that side is full, I find dish towels, wipe everything dry, and find cupboard space to put it all away.

I'm still at this chore when Miss Frankie comes from the bedroom. She feels the water in the big pot and says she needs some clean towels.

I open a drawer and hand her several dish towels. How is she? I ask.

No fever, fortunately. She's rid herself before, and she'll do it again if she has to. Miss Frankie doesn't say rid of what, and I don't ask.

Together we carry the big pot of heated water into the bedroom and set it on a kitchen chair Miss Frankie has brought in. Mrs. Cole is sitting on another chair next to the bed, her hands covering her face. Her shoulders are shaking, so I know she's crying. Miss Frankie keeps whispering over and over: there, there, Linda, now, now Linda.

Miss Frankie has taken the sheets off the bed and dumped them on the floor. I help her fold the quilts and set them atop the bureau. She motions for me to take the sheets. She tells me to find a washtub and set the sheets to soak under the outside faucet. Keep the water running, she says.

When I get back, Mrs. Cole is still sitting on the chair, now holding a wet dish towel over her face, but she seems to have stopped crying. Miss Frankie and I together turn the mattress over. The other side is only better because it is dry.

Linda, where do you keep sheets? Miss Frankie asks. And Mrs. Cole nods her head toward the bureau.

I open the top drawer and find a clean nightgown and hand it to Miss Frankie. In the next drawer down, I find a set of ironed sheets and pillow slips edged with embroidery. I'm surprised to find such daintiness in this household. Miss Frankie and I remake the bed.

As Miss Frankie starts to help Mrs. Cole out of her soiled nightgown, she whispers to me to finish up in the kitchen. As I work, I occasionally glance behind me as Miss Frankie washes Mrs. Cole from the big pot of warm water. The house does not have a bathtub, just a small room with a chamber pot for those who can't make it all the way to the outhouse, like if it's raining hard or thundering or freezing outside. For bathing, I suppose they stand at the kitchen sink and use a rag on face, necks, underarms, and privates.

I hurry through cleaning the kitchen while Miss Frankie helps Mrs. Cole into her clean bed and covers her with a quilt. I'll bring you a bite to eat, Miss Frankie tells her. She hands me the soiled nightgown.

I go out to check on the sheets and see if the water has begun to run clear. I slip the nightgown into the water to soak. Then I find a small stool, a washboard, a bar of yellow soap, and set to scrubbing. I had often watched Miss Frankie scrub stubborn stains against a washboard, so it is like I'd always known how.

When I'm trying to wring out the sheets, I see Mr. Cole and his boys carrying hoes and tools into the barn. And suddenly Arnold is right there next to me, so close he gives me a fright. He takes the sheet from me and wrings it out and hands it back to me, then wrings out the other one. He helps me pin them to the line.

His work-stained hands have left marks on the clean sheets. He sees that and seems to be trying to say he's sorry, the words coming out with great effort. My wet skirt is hugging my legs. My arms are limp. And suddenly, damnit, I think my heart will break. I am ready for this particular summer to be over.

Chapter 16
Uncle Luke's Ice Cream

A letter from Miss Frankie warns us that Uncle Luke's illness is serious. The medicines no longer work and nothing he eats has made him any better. So, he gets taken to the hospital in Jacksonville for an operation on his gallbladder, but when they open him up, they find he is full of cancer. All they can do was sew him back up.

Soon after, Miss Frankie calls to tell us Uncle Luke insists he isn't about to die at Nan Travis, the Jacksonville hospital, so they let Dr. Hart carry him home.

Mama and I leave that very afternoon and Mark comes with us. I bring along schoolbooks, but reading in the car makes me carsick. Mostly we talk in low voices so whoever is in the back seat can rest while waiting their turn to drive. Not me. Although I can drive Daddy Lee's pickup, I do not have a real driver's license.

When Mark's driving and my mama's asleep in the back seat, I ask him how doctors can be so stupid and not know Uncle Luke has cancer. Mark explains a doctor is a lot like a car mechanic, only without all the proper tools or a complete instruction manual. Most doctors, he says, do not have Miss Frankie's gift for making people well.

We drive all night and arrive mid-morning at Dr. Hart's where one side of the front room is fitted out with a hospital bed. Uncle Luke is asleep. He's wearing a hospital gown printed with small flying ducks. Aunt Mae is sitting next to his bed and petting his hand. She gets up and goes with my mama to the sofa on the far side of the room. They sit with their heads together, whispering. Mark goes to the kitchen with Dr. Hart so they can talk doctor stuff.

I sit on the window seat across from Uncle Luke's bed. Spring has arrived down here. I watch a pair of blackbirds high stepping around on the spiky lawn of St. Augustine.

After a while, Uncle Luke starts groaning and rocking himself from side to side. Aunt Mae and my mama get up and come over. Aunt Mae hushes him softly and my mama pulls the covers up and tucks them around his shoulders. He quiets and Aunt Mae and my mama go back to the sofa.

I go back to watching the blackbirds. Through the bottom part of the window glass, wavy with age, the birds' high, careful steps make me think of wading birds with the muck and mud of some pond edge sucking and pulling at their feet.

Frankie, Frankie! Uncle Luke's cries bring everyone to his bedside. Mark and Dr. Hart come from the kitchen.

He's dreaming, Dr. Hart says. It's the pain killers.
Uncle Luke hasn't opened his eyes. He still doesn't know we are all here. His raised knees have lifted the sheet into a tent and beneath the flap of it I can see his shriveled up private parts. I turn my eyes back to the window.

When Uncle Luke settles himself, Dr. Hart tells my mama to go on home and take me and Aunt Mae with her, and to ask Miss

Frankie to come sit with Uncle Luke a while, if she can. Mark, he says, can stay here. Mrs. Hart is already fixing the back bedroom for him.

He was calling for Miss Frankie, I tell Jewel. We're putting fresh sheets on all the beds as we don't know who might be coming to stay over. Jewel says we might as well be ready. My mama decided to stay with Aunt Mae at her house.

How come he was calling for Miss Frankie, I ask, and not for Aunt Mae, them still being sorta sweethearts?

Jewel finishes stuffing a pillow into a pillow slip. Maybe there's a certain specialness between a brother and a sister. Maybe the memory of some kind of perfect way of getting along. She sits down on the side of the bed and hugs the pillow to herself.

I sit down next to her. Me and JP seem more like brother and sister than cousins, I say. Still, I can't imagine I'm gonna be calling for him when I lay dying.

Jewel smothers her laughter in the pillow, and I try to smother mine behind my hands. It is probably the exact minute Uncle Luke died.

The annual spring cleaning has recently cleared the weeds and swept the grave mounds. The leaves of all the trees and bushes are a pale, fresh green, and the old rose bushes are just putting out the first blooms of the season. Every relative I can think of has showed up, even some of Uncle Luke's and Miss Frankie's from down around Beaumont, ones I have never met before.

Aunt Mae's face is blotchy from crying. All the ladies are keeping hankies handy. Cousin Valentine is wearing that black velvet hat with the face veil, proving she leaves it at the house on purpose, so she has it when she needs it for funerals.

There's no church service as there's no reason. Uncle Luke hardly ever saw the inside of a church when he was alive. The preacher talks on and on, saying what a wonderful person Uncle Luke was, even though the preacher's likely never met him. Then he starts in on The Lord is My Shepherd.

Aunt Mae is hanging onto my mama's arm and a fresh set of tears start flowing. Her shoulders shake so hard her hat falls off. She looks so pitiful everyone else starts back to crying. My mama picks up the hat, dusts it off, and sets it back on Aunt Mae's head.

And then my mama surprises everyone by singing Amazing Grace. Now everyone is weeping, even my mama, singing with tears falling down her face. She was already a spectacle with her string of pearls, her fancy black silk dress, and black patent slingbacks. No telling what people thought of that fancy get-up. I guess I hadn't thought at all, so I'm wearing scruffy penny loafers and one of Jewel's dresses, a navy blue thing polka-dotted with tiny white stars and cinched around with my jeans belt.

When the praying is over and everyone's just standing around talking, Jewel sidles over to me. Your young doctor can't take his eyes off you, she whispers.

You're crazy, I whisper back, looking over to where Mark is standing with Dr. and Mrs. Hart with her beautiful waterfall of white hair. Mark and I exchange small smiles.

See, Jewel says, he's coming over. And she leaves to stand with JP and his daddy who are standing with Uncle Lum and Aunt Bessie. I watch Jewel push JP's hair out of his eyes and him try to swing his head away from her. Then I see her slip her arm through Charlie Henderson's and Aunt Bessie's eyes nearly bugout of her face. I figure Jewel is just playing with her.

Mark comes over, but he doesn't say anything. Aunt Mae has started making some kind of commotion. She is so heartbroken

I'm afraid she's gonna try to throw herself into the grave on top of Uncle Luke's coffin.

Come, I tell Mark, and he follows me over to the Walker graves that are somewhat in the shade. I perch myself on Herman Alsop Walker's tombstone, cross my legs and blow my nose.

I just can't, Aunt Mae is saying to Miss Frankie. I won't, she says, flinging her arm toward her own family's graves. I'll drown myself in the Neches and then y'all won't have a body to bury.

Aunt Mae and my real grandma were sisters, I explain to Mark, but evidently my aunt doesn't want to be buried with her own family.

Does it have to be decided now? Mark asks.

Actually, this is a good time, I say. Seeing as everyone's here. Witnesses, you know.

Miss Frankie has her hands on her hips and is looking around, studying things. Alright, she says. Mae can be on one side, and I'll be on the other. She turns to Daddy Lee. I know you have a place for me, you lying between me and Rosetta, but Mae can't be next to Luke all by herself. It wouldn't be proper, them not ever being married.

Rosetta, Mark says. Is that who you were named for? Is that your real name?

I nod.

And JP?

Jackson Parker. Named for someone related to his daddy. They're well-known families in these parts.

We all wait and watch as Daddy Lee studies the burial problem. He stares at the ground and jiggles the keys and coins in his pocket. Finally, he nods his head in agreement.

Back at the house, all the leaves have been added to the dining table and two card tables added, making it stretch from the piano all the way out through the French doors and onto the bricks of the side porch.

Daddy Lee slices the ham, while fried chicken, side dishes, and hot rolls are passed. The things that were decided that day were such that I don't think a day goes by for the rest of our lives that someone isn't reminded of Uncle Luke's funeral.

First, my mama decides Aunt Mae should come to live with us in Iowa. She said she realized it the moment she reached down to pick up Aunt Mae's hat and dusted it off. Aunt Mae needs someone to care for now that Uncle Luke is gone. She can come up north and take care of us.

Then there is Jewel who decides to close her beauty shop. She says looking at Mrs. Hart made her realize how ancient all her ladies were getting to be. Anyway, she has always wanted a hardware store. So, her putting her arm through Charlie Henderson's at the cemetery wasn't to tease Aunt Bessie, but because Charlie Henderson is the loan officer at the bank.

Jewel was wrong about Mark making eyes at me. He was merely busting to tell me Dr. Hart offered to let him take over his practice after Mark finishes med school and residency.

The table is so full that me and JP take our plates over to the low table in front of the sofa where Daddy Lee naps. From there, we can watch the others. Nobody brought children as no one wants a car trip with young'uns if it isn't absolutely necessary.

At the big table there is Miss Frankie and Daddy Lee, the preacher and his wife, Dr. and Mrs. Hart, my mama and Mark, Jewel and Charlie Henderson, Uncle Lum and Aunt Bessie, the relatives from down around Beaumont, Uncle Walt and Aunt Suzette who only ever visit once in a blue moon, Uncle Hoke who has the sawmill on the road to Athens and his wife Lucille, Cousin Valentine and her husband, Richard. In all I count more than twenty people squeezed at that table, and everyone talking, telling funny stories about Uncle Luke and laughing.

Richard is pleased to sit at the far end, out on the porch, because being outside means he can keep his hat on. Later he and Charlie Henderson are the main crankers of the ice cream maker. Miss Frankie used peaches from the freezer for the ice cream custard. I know Uncle Luke would have really enjoyed his own funeral; especially as peach ice cream was his very favorite.

EPILOGUE

When I was 10, almost 11, I left Texas and did not return until almost 40 years later. I was fifteen, when my grandparents came to visit us in California. We were renting a grand Victorian house with orange groves on two sides. In my book I loaned this house and its interiors to the up-north grandmother.

During their visit, Daddy Lee asked me to sit with him a while in the parlor, a formal room we rarely used. The sofa was slip-covered in white linen, a rather silly extravagance of my mother's, given that we were a family of eight children. Side by side we sat. He took my hand, and as he held it, he told me he thought he did not have much longer to live. Then he retrieved a small piece of paper from his pocket and gave it to me. He had written: I love you Mick (my childhood nickname).

He died about two years later. My mother flew to Texas for the funeral. Less than 10 years after, Miss Frankie moved into the local nursing home. She and I had corresponded for several years, and I still have her letters. She told me she had gotten lonely, especially during the long winters when she could not garden. She sent me a photo of herself with a group of residents and told me she had gone to kindergarten with many of them, including her best childhood friend. When she died, I had just sent her a dozen yellow roses for her birthday.

In this book, which is an autofiction (IOW a fake memoir), none of the other characters were real, although I imagined a history for each of them. Vesta, Etta's mother, only returned for her parents' funerals. When Aunt Mae died, she was buried up north, so Miss Frankie was buried next to Daddy Lee, with his first wife on his other side.

Jewel opened a hardware store where JP helped after school. He went on to the junior college in Tyler, taking an associate degree in accounting. He set up an office where he kept the books for many of the town's small businesses. He married a local girl who taught school for a few years before they had kids. Charlie Henderson, JP's father, remarried. Jewel never did.

After finishing med school, Mark took over Dr Hart's practice. He enjoyed general practice, getting to know his patients' extended family medical histories.

Etta attended college up north and became an architect. She specialized in the design of small lake cabins. Her skills were in demand in Texas where the number of new reservoir lakes grew by the hundreds. Of course, she returned.

ABOUT THE AUTHOR

Mitchell Hagerstrom was born in Iowa City and now lives on Maryland's Eastern Shore. She has lived in Texas, Virginia, North Carolina, California, Hawaii, Japan, Missouri, Louisiana, and Micronesia. Most of these locales appear in her fictions. Mitchell had studied writing in college and published her first novel "Miss Gone-Overseas" in 2012.

OTHER WORKS BY MITCHELL HAGERSTROM

"MISS GON-OVERSEAS" Pillow Book 1st Edition
published by Tiny Toe Press 2012, 2nd Edition published by
Penryn Editions 2019.

'GATHERED PIECES", collection of 19 short narratives
and poems published by Penryn Press 2019.

"OVERSEAS STORIES", prequel or sequel to Miss
Gone-Overseas, short stories, e-book version published by Tiny
Toe Press 2012, 2nd Edition paperback and e-book published
by Penryn Press 2019.